COMPANY OFFICE

SURPLUS

The Company Store

LOIS LENSKI—1958

COAL CAMP GIRL

Other Books by Lois Lenski

Autobiographical
> A Little Girl of Nineteen Hundred

Historical
> Phebe Fairchild, Her Book
> A-Going to the Westward
> Bound Girl of Cobble Hill
> Ocean-Born Mary
> Indian Captive
> Blueberry Corners
> Puritan Adventure

Regional
> Bayou Suzette
> Strawberry Girl
> Blue Ridge Billy
> Judy's Journey
> Boom Town Boy
> Cotton in My Sack
> Texas Tomboy
> Prairie School
> Mama Hattie's Girl
> Corn Farm Boy
> San Francisco Boy
> Flood Friday
> Houseboat Girl

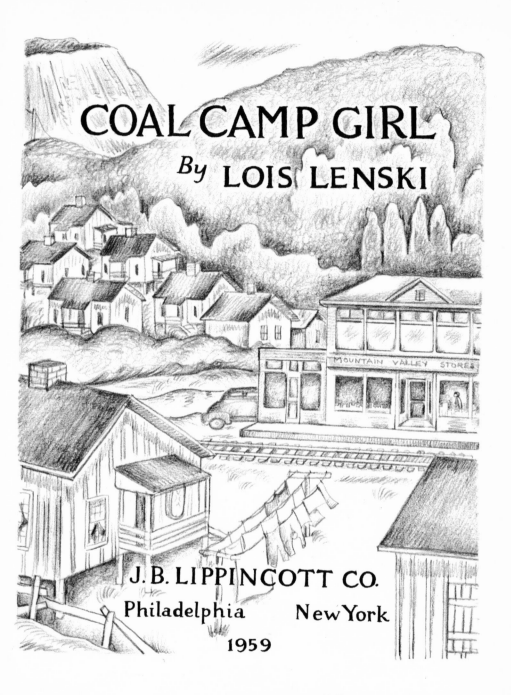

COAL CAMP GIRL
By LOIS LENSKI

J. B. LIPPINCOTT CO.

Philadelphia   New York

1959

To
my beloved
coal camp children

Foreword

To write of the beautiful mountains of West Virginia and to share the lives of the people, especially the many children who live in their shadows, has been a rare privilege. To enter into the experiences of the miners' families for even a short time, to share their hardships and hazards, their courage and their blind faith in an unknown future, has been truly enriching for me.

There is sadness and sorrow in their lives, but there is joy and gladness too. Even as the slate-blackened hill stands out like a sore thumb in contrast to the lush greenness and beauty of the mountainside, so sadness makes a dark dent in the happiness we are all heir to but never attain.

For some of us the battle is soon over, easily won. For others, for the coal miner and his family, the struggle may be never-ending. But on he goes, despite setbacks that would dishearten most of us, never sorry for himself, always smiling and cheerful, for this is "the life he knows." Despite the drama in the life of every coal miner, which none can escape, there is a smile on his lips and hope in his heart. Knowing him and his children has touched me deeply.

Coal is the miners' life. They hate it and yet they love it, for they cannot live without it. With blind faith, they face a future when the coal may be used up, or rest secure in a fond hope that Nature's bounty is inexhaustible, no matter how greedy man may become or how devastating his clutches since he has armed himself with vulture-like machinery. Some run away from it, escape to other things, but most are slaves in bondage to it from birth to death. Coal strikes back sometimes, the miner stumblers and falters, but always gets up again, pressing onward.

My own experiences in the coal region were exciting and tre-mendous. I talked to management, inspectors, owners and miners alike. I rode on a coal car to the inside of a mine where the men were working and talked to them there. I would not have wanted to write this story if I had not had this deeply moving experience. I tried to see and feel for myself during a short interval the under-ground environment where the miners spend their lives.

I studied the miners' faces as I watched them enter and leave the mines, or as I met them in company store or on the street. They were always cordial and friendly, willing to answer my many ques-tions. I spent days with the children in a coal camp school and with the upper grades in a town school. They shared with me their ex-citements and adventures, and confided their worries, their fears and their needs. Through all their tales ran a strong thread of courage and hope. As far as I was able to, I tried to project myself into their dramatic and hazardous lives, and to see life from their point of view, not my own.

I loved the coal children. Coal is their life from the moment their eyes open until they close them at the end. Coal heats them, clothes and shelters them, feeds them, provides their all. The coal camp children know well the foreboding sound of the long drawn-out mine whistle and the dreaded shriek of an ambulance galloping down the hill, sounds which strike terror to the heart of the child as well as the mother. They live through the long hours of tense waiting, too, hoping, often in vain, for a possible miracle. Far too many of them know the pinch of want and the pain of hunger, caused more often than not by their parents' perennial improvi-dence. But even so, with the natural resilience of childhood, the boys can fight and ride each other piggyback and the girls in circles play In and Out the Window *and other time-honored games of childhood.*

I am grateful to Miss Wilma Brown, Librarian of the Kanawha County Public Library, Charleston, West Virginia, for her generous help; and to friends, teachers, parents and children in the Oak Hill area of West Virginia for sharing their ideas, information and experiences with me; also to the West Virginia Department of Mines and several state mine inspectors for suggestions. I wish to thank also the school children in Shallmar, Maryland, Colver, Pennsylvania, and Beaverdale, Pennsylvania for their letters and kindly efforts to interest me in their locality. All the incidents described in this book are true—including that of the three lost boys,—and have happened in real life to living people in the area.

For fifteen years I have been wanting to write this book. Suddenly, after many setbacks, the way opened and I saw the pathway ahead to this particular location, which I visited in person in September and October 1958. I am happy to add a coal camp story to my series of Regional America books.

Lois Lenski

Lutean Shores, Tarpon Springs, Florida
January 1959

DEFINITIONS

Bank clothes, bank hat, etc.—the word "bank" evidently derives from "coal bank."

Crib-blocks—short timbers set in crisscross fashion, tower-like; used where a single post would not be strong enough to hold up the roof headers.

Cross-cut—a passageway for ventilation.

Drift mine—a mine entered from the side of a hill instead of a vertical shaft.

Drift-mouth—entrance to a drift mine.

Entry—mine opening.

Face—working part of the coal mine; wall where the coal is being cut, shot down and loaded.

Header—a cross timber 4 x 8 x 12 ft. set on posts to hold rock roof up.

Main haulageway, or hallway—passage through which the coal is hauled out.

Man-trip—a train of coal cars fitted with seats which carried the miners from the portal along the haulageway to the sections where they work, and brings them out again at the end of the shift.

Motor—electric locomotive which pulls coal cars in and out.

Portal—mine opening.

Portal-to-portal pay—the miner's work-day begins when he enters the portal; he is paid for his time beginning when he enters the portal and ending when he comes out to the portal at end of shift.

Punch mines—mines that are opened up along strip mine highwalls and extend several hundred feet underground, employing from three to five men.

Runway—a track or path.

Scrip—artificial money advanced by the coal company to miners on credit.

Scrip-card—a card on which the miner's advances are recorded.

Stump—a large block of coal left between two rooms.

Tipple—place where coal is dumped or loaded; apparatus by which loaded coal cars are emptied by tipping.

Trip—a train of mine cars.

MY DADDY DIGS COAL

WORDS BY LOIS LENSKI

MUSIC BY CLYDE ROBERT BULLA

Un-der the moun-tain, Un-der the hill, My dad-dy goes to work With his
Un-der the ci-ty, Un-der the town, The mine— is a cave Hol-lowel
Un-der the moun-tain Un-der the hill My dad-dy goes to work With his

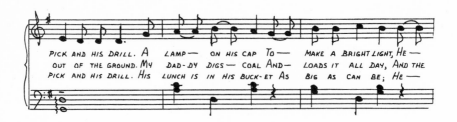

pick and his drill. A lamp— on his cap To— make a bright light, He—
out of the ground. My dad-dy digs— coal And— loads it all day, And the
pick and his drill. His lunch is in his buck-et As big as can be; He—

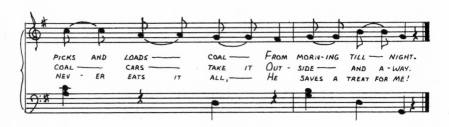

picks and loads— coal— From morn-ing till— night.
coal— cars— take it Out— side— and a-way.
nev-er eats it all,— He saves a treat for me!

Copyright 1957 by Lois Lenski and Clyde Robert Bulla

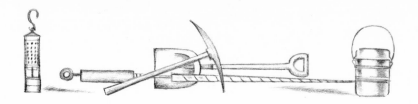

Contents

1. Bucket . . . . . . *page* 1
2. Coal 15
3. Payday 31
4. Hardship 53
5. Pony 71
6. Winter 86
7. Disaster 102
8. Summer 122
9. Lost 133
10. Rescue 150
11. Wedding 165

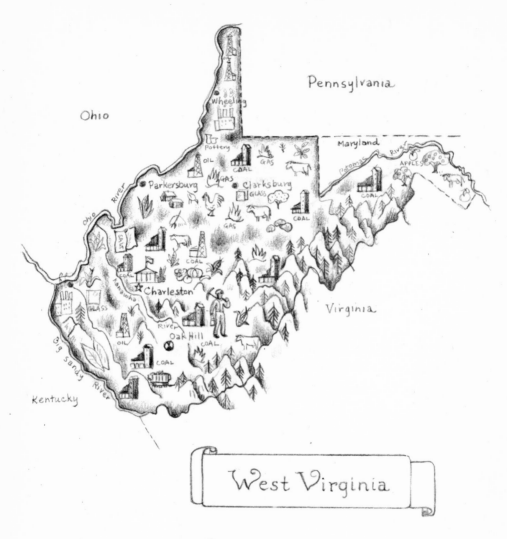

Ohio

Pennsylvania

Wheeling

Maryland

Pottery
OIL
COAL GAS

Parkersburg
GAS
Clarksburg
GLASS

Potomac River
APPLES
COAL

COAL

Ohio River

COAL

GAS

COAL

Kanawha River

Charleston

GLASS

Virginia

River
Oak Hill
COAL

OIL

Big Sandy River

COAL

Kentucky

West Virginia

⊗ Location of Story

COAL CAMP GIRL

Chapter One

BUCKET

"Mama, what time is it?"

Tina ran up on the back porch.

"Almost three-thirty," said her mother. "There's the whistle now."

The sharp blast of the mine whistle echoed through the valley.

"Time to meet Daddy," said the little girl. "I'm going now."

Mama came out on the porch. She held up her hand to shade her eyes from the afternoon sun. She looked across the railroad track, where the large black coal-tipple stood.

"I see the men coming out," she said.

But Tina was already flying down the road on feet as light as wings. She looked back once and saw Mama take the large oval tin tub down from its hook on the wall. That was for Daddy's bath. Some of the miners went straight to the company bathhouse, but they had to pay extra for that. So Daddy always came home black. He said he liked to take his bath at home.

Christina Wilson was nine years old. She ran fast, her short hair flying loose in the wind. What would Daddy have for a treat today? Maybe it would be something special!

"Tina! Tina! Wait for me!" a voice called behind her.

"Oh, that Ronnie!" Tina slowed up. "Why does he always have to tag along?"

Little feet came pattering up and there was her brother Ronnie. Ronnie was only five and had brown hair like Tina's. His clothes were ragged and dirty.

"Why can't you stay at home?" asked Tina. "I thought you were sleeping."

"You ran away from me," said Ronnie, almost crying

"Why do you have to come?" asked Tina.

"I want Daddy's bucket," said Ronnie.

"It's my turn today," said Tina. "I'll get there first." She ran on ahead.

There came the miners with their swinging buckets up the dirt road from the mine. They were talking and laughing as they walked along. Tina looked at them as they walked by. With their faces so black, all the men looked alike. Only their voices were different.

"Where's my girl? Did she come for me today?"

That was Daddy. His voice was big and booming. The next minute he had stepped behind her. Then Tina felt a hand on her face—a big black hand! She pulled it off, she knew it was Daddy's.

"Don't make me black!" she cried, laughing.

Other little girls came running to meet their black daddies, and were scrambling for their buckets. Every miner's child was looking for a treat. This was an age-old tradition in all mining camps.

Walter Wilson was a strong husky man of fifty, with a full face and a genial smile. He wore his bank clothes, his hard-shell bank cap, leather jacket and his mine shoes with the hard copper toes. He had been a coal miner all his life, for he had entered the mines as a boy of twelve. He loved the work for he knew no other.

Tina and Ronnie tugged at Daddy's bucket.

"I got it first!" cried Ronnie.

"I came first," said Tina. "He tagged after me."

"Now here, no scrapping," said Daddy. "There's a treat for you both."

The children never knew what they were going to get. But whatever it was, the food had a different taste just because it came from the mine.

Daddy opened the round aluminum bucket. It was made in two parts like a double boiler. The bottom part held two or three quarts of drinking water. That was why it was so big. If Daddy was ever trapped in the mine and could not get out for a few days, the water might save his life. The top half of the bucket, called the "deck" held his lunch. Daddy lifted the cover himself and the two children peered in. The sandwiches were gone, the pie was gone, the apple was gone, but there, hiding under the waxed paper, were two sticks of chewing gum.

"Gum!" cried Ronnie. "Goody!"

"Peppermint!" said Tina. "Oh, Daddy!"

The next minute the wrappers were off and the two children were chewing gum. They took hold of Daddy's hands and started happily for home.

The Wilsons lived in Linden, a West Virginia coal camp. "Coal camp" is the local name for a coal-mining town. Linden lay in a deep valley with high mountains on all sides, and was cut in two by Arbutus Creek and the railroad track. In the center of the valley, over the tracks, was the coal-tipple, a tall black structure which looked like a great coal bin standing on stilts. Two drift mines opened into the mountains on either side of the tipple. Only one was operating, and that only part time. Daddy said he was lucky to have a job.

The camp was filled with houses built by the coal company many years before, set together in rows on different levels. Some of the houses were boarded up and empty, where people had moved out when the mines began to close down, some to homes of their own elsewhere or to other occupations. There were yards and fences, and in a few yards flowers were blooming. Twenty-five years ago the houses had been painted white, but now were looking dingy and gray, blackened by coal dust over the years. Out by every fence was a small coal shed with a high window into which coal could be shoveled from a truck. All the houses in the camp were heated by coal.

Daddy knew everybody in town. He called hello or nodded his head to people he saw as they walked along. Men sat on the little narrow porches now, their tired feet resting on the railing. Women called children to come in and eat supper. As the sun sank behind Laurel Mountain on the west, the shadow of dusk fell across the camp. Daddy and the children came to the last house on the narrow street.

"Number 181—that's us!" said Tina. "If I didn't know our number, I might go in the wrong house—they're all alike."

Daddy sniffed. "I smell beef stew cooking."

A three-foot porch was on the front close to the road. As they walked around the side of the house to the back, a short-haired brown dog came out to meet them.

"Hi, Queenie!" said Daddy, stooping to pat her on the head. "No, I didn't save you a treat, old girl."

"Here's Daddy, Mama!"

Tina opened the back door and they all went in.

"Got my bath about ready?" asked Daddy.

"As soon as Jeff brings the cold water," said Mama. "Do you want to eat first?"

Tina's big sister, Celia, age nineteen, stood by the stove stirring food in a stew pan. She held her year-old baby on her arm. Celia was the Wilsons' married daughter. Her husband had been in the Air Force and was killed overseas, so she lived at home.

"Dinner's about ready," said Celia.

Walter Wilson went over and tickled the baby under the chin. "How's Letty?" he asked.

"Fussy today," said Celia. "She's teething again. She won't let me alone for a minute."

"Where's Jeff?" asked Daddy.

"He's coming," called Tina.

At the outdoor spigot in a neighbor's yard, her brother Jeff had filled two buckets with water. One spigot was shared by four houses. The boy came up the back steps with the water, the dog Queenie at his heels. Mama started pouring hot water from the stove into the big oval bath tub. She had spread newspapers on the floor underneath.

As Daddy took off his jacket and his shirt, coal dust fell from his clothes. The pockets were full of coal dust. Mama took his clothes out on the porch and shook them.

"Stay on the newspapers, Walter," she said. "I get tired of mopping the floor every night."

"Hi, Dad," said Jeff, as he came in.

"Hi, son," said Daddy. "Got your chores all done?"

"Not yet, Daddy," said Jeff. "Got to get coal in next."

"Don't wait till it's dark," said Daddy.

"I stopped at Uncle Chick's on the way home," said Jeff. "He brought Snowball home from the mine. Poor pony— she'd hurt her foot. We both looked at it but couldn't see what was wrong."

"Maybe she just needs new shoes," said Daddy.

"Uncle Chick's going to have her shod before he works her again," said Jeff. "I took her up to Grandpa Ferris's."

"If he keeps her in the pasture a couple of days, likely she'll be all right," said Daddy.

"Oh, is Snowball up at Grandpa's?" cried Tina. "Can I go up and ride her?"

Jeff looked at his sister and frowned. "You can't ride a pony with a hurt foot."

"But you said there was nothing wrong with it . . ." began Tina. "Snowball's a nice pony. Daddy, can't I have her for a pet?"

"Snowball's a work pony, not a pet," said Daddy. "She's worth three hundred and fifty dollars."

"Shoo! Shoo! You kids get out of the kitchen," said Mama. "Daddy wants to take his bath. Supper's ready and we'll eat as soon as he's done."

Grandpa Ferris was Mama's daddy. Mama had two brothers, Chick and Jack. Uncle Chick leased several small punch mines. They used ponies to work them. Grandpa and Grandma Ferris lived up on the high road by Laurel Mountain, above the coal camp. Grandpa had a pasture there, where he kept the ponies when they were not working. Uncle Jack was not married and still lived with his parents. Uncle Chick was married to Aunt Effie and they had three children, Trig, Dede and Cindy. They lived in Crabapple Hollow on the other side of Laurel Mountain.

Supper was over, the dishes were washed and put away, when Uncle Chick and Uncle Jack came over in Uncle Jack's car. Tina and Ronnie took Uncle Jack by the hand, but he shook them off and sat down to talk to the men.

"Run along, kids," he said. "I want to talk to your dad."

"Still working, Walter?" asked Uncle Chick.

Daddy nodded.

"They laid off twenty men today," said Uncle Jack, "but not me and not Walter."

"Your turns are coming," said Uncle Chick. "Linden Number 3 is worked out. You boys had better come in with us and do strip mining. Grandpa's got a good lease from the company, and we get a sure price for every ton we dig. It's like piece work—what you produce, you get paid for."

"That's O.K.," said Daddy. "But I've been working for

the Mountain Valley Coal Company all my life. Guess I'll stick by them."

"I feel the same way, Walter," said Jack. "Chick wants me to go in with him on this pony mine, but I like the big mine better."

"Until they lay you off, and then where'll you be?" said Chick.

"When the company gets more coal orders in, they'll take the men back on again," said Daddy. "I've always liked the Mountain Valley Coal Company. Back in 1937 or 1938, Linden Number 4 dumped 39,999 tons of coal in a single day—one ton lacking forty thousand. In the thirties they employed fifteen hundred men and there were six thousand people living in Linden."

"And look at it now," said Uncle Chick. "A little old run-down camp with a handful of people. You always like to brag about the good old days. They're over now and that coal's gone. The little that's left, the company can't afford to use their big machinery on. So they lease it to us."

"Yes—the leavin's," said Daddy. "That's what you and Gramp are diggin', with your little old ponies."

"But we're independent!" said Uncle Chick.

"I'll stick by the company," said Daddy, "as long as they need me."

"Me too," said Jack. "I don't want to go back to pick and shovel."

No one said anything for a while. Then the boy Jeff spoke up.

"Uncle Chick, will you give me a job in your punch mine when I get a little older?"

"Sure thing!" said Uncle Chick. "That is, if there's any coal left. Let's see, you're about twelve now . . ."

"Next June," said Jeff.

"You've only got six more years to wait," laughed Uncle Chick. "The law now says you've got to be eighteen."

"Wish I could start at twelve like Daddy did," said Jeff. "Bet I could drive the ponies right now—better than old Okey Travis. He whips 'em, that makes 'em mean."

"Ponies are just like children," said Mama. "If you go yelling and slashing them around, they get hard-headed and never are any good."

"I keep telling Okey every day not to use his whip," said Uncle Chick. "He knows better but loses his temper sometimes."

"I'd be a better pony-driver than he is," said Jeff. "He should never have whipped old Smokey. Smokey killed a man once when he whipped him with a whip. But when I took care of him, there couldn't nobody handle him but me. There couldn't nobody ride him but me. He wouldn't go to anybody dressed in black."

"Jeff's right," said Daddy. "Jeff's got a way with them ponies. He can get 'em to do whatever he wants, without any trouble, just by coaxing and sweet-talkin'.'"

Jeff's pale face glowed as he talked of the pony he had loved and lost.

"He was smoke-colored," said Jeff, remembering. "He was the same color as Trigger, Roy Rogers' horse. He was forty-six inches, came up just chest high, to the second button on my shirt. . . . I hated it when he had to be killed . . . and you burned him up . . ." The boy's voice broke.

"Who told you we did that?" asked Uncle Chick sternly.

"I saw it," said Jeff. "I watched it. I was hiding in the bushes."

No one spoke for a time.

"It's the law, son," said Daddy slowly. "You got to dispose of the carcass in a sanitary way."

"Oh, but you should see Bright Eyes!" said Uncle Chick, in an effort to change the subject. "You'll like Bright Eyes . . ."

"You've got a *new* pony called *Bright Eyes?*" asked Tina, eagerly.

"Yes, we rode clear over to Virginia and bought two new ponies," said Uncle Chick. "Their names are Bright Eyes and Diamond."

Tina clapped her hands. "What pretty names! Oh, I want to ride Bright Eyes. Will he be staying at Gramp's? Can I have him for a pet?"

"Yes, until we start to work him," said Uncle Chick. "You wouldn't want Diamond—he's pretty wild."

"Mama, can I go spend the night at Grandma's?" asked Tina.

"Not tonight, it's way past your bedtime," said Mama. "It's too late to be ridin' ponies. Ronnie's sound asleep. You go and hop in and be quick about it. Jeff, time for bed."

Soon the children called good night and Mama switched off the bedroom lights.

One by one the lights went out in the little houses, and darkness covered the little coal camp in the valley.

Chapter Two

COAL

"Hɪ, Uɴᴄʟᴇ Jᴀᴄᴋ!" called the children.

Tina and Jeff ran to meet him as he drove up in his car. Uncle Jack was their favorite uncle. He was young and good-natured, and made a fuss over the children.

"Jack, you'd better get my house coal before snow flies," said Mama. "Winter will be here before we know it."

"No time like the present," said Uncle Jack. He turned to the children. "Want to go for a ride?"

"Yes, yes." Tina and Jeff jumped in the car.

Daddy and Uncle Jack were not working today. The whistle did not blow at six the night before, and that meant the mine would not operate today. The men had only three days of steady work a week now.

"We'll get some house coal for your mother," said Uncle Jack. "I've got some tubs and sacks in the back trunk."

The car went chugging down the road, with the children bouncing in the back seat. But instead of going up the mountain, Uncle Jack drove down past the big tipple and parked near the entrance to Linden Number 3 mine.

"We can't get coal here," said Jeff.

"No," said Uncle Jack. "We'll go up on the mountain later. I have to get something first. Want me to show you around?"

Tina had never been there before. Uncle Jack pointed out the lamp house, the bathhouse and the mine foreman's office. In the office, he showed them the fire boss's reports, time sheets and injury charts. On the wall was a large map of the mine interior, with all hallways, break-throughs and cross-cuts marked. Uncle Jack told the children the mine was laid out like a big city, with main streets, side streets and alleys. He showed them where his section was working—three miles into the side of the mountain, directly under the town of Mapleton.

Then they came out and went into the lamp house. They saw all the miners' lamps hanging up for recharging. They saw the board with numbered hooks for the miners' identification checks. Uncle Jack gave Tina and Jack each a bank camp with a light. He fastened the batteries to their belts.

"Now I'm a miner!" cried Jeff. "Give me a pick and a shovel!"

"Oh, the battery's heavy," said Tina. "Don't you get tired carrying it all day long?"

Uncle Jack laughed. "No," he said. "I'm so used to it, I never notice it. Come along with me."

"Where are we going?" asked Tina timidly.

"I have to do a little work inside," said Uncle Jack. "Want to go along?"

"Sure!" said Jeff. "All the way in?"

"Can I go too?" asked Tina. She had never been allowed to go near the big mine before. "Will it hurt me?"

"Of course not," said Uncle Jack. "It might be good for you to see how your daddy and Uncle Jack have to go under the ground where it is dark to make a living."

"I've been in plenty of mines before," bragged Jeff. "I'm going to be a miner when I grow up."

"Keep your lamps on then," said Uncle Jack, "and come along. Just be careful and go only where I tell you to. See that overhead wire? Don't walk under it. That's a live wire strung along the ceiling. It carries the electricity for the trolley which runs the train of coal cars in and out. The electric engine that pulls it is called a motor. When the men ride the 'man-trip' to go in to work, they sit on only one side of the car, so no one will be under the live wire. That's for safety."

All her life Tina had wanted to go inside a mine, to see where Daddy worked, but now that she had the chance, she was not so sure she wanted to go.

"Do we have to walk?" she asked. "Is it a long way?"

"We'll walk first," said Jeff, "but pretty soon we'll crawl."

"Crawl?" asked Tina.

"Yes, when we get to the low coal," said Jeff.

Tina clung tightly to Uncle Jack's hand as they went in.

They walked upright in the main hall, then Uncle Jack had to bend over, and finally even the children had to go on hands and knees. Uncle Jack kept talking as Jeff asked questions, but Tina paid little attention.

"Cousin Trig and I went in Sunrise Mine once," said Jeff. "We pretended we were miners. We found an old mine car and pushed it in. We pretended to load it. We rode the motor and played it broke down and we had to fix it."

"You stay out of the abandoned mines," said Uncle Jack. "The law requires that the drift-mouth be closed so people and animals can't get in. Don't ever let Trig take you in an old mine again, Jeff. There might be pockets of gas in some of those old working places, and it would kill you. It's very dangerous."

They came to Uncle Jack's section.

"Here we are right under Mapleton dime store!" laughed Uncle Jack. "Now wait a minute till I find my tools."

Tina let go of Uncle Jack's hand. She heard him explaining to Jeff about the coal saws and noisy electric drills that loosen the coal by blasting, and the "joy" machine that loads it. Uncle Jack's work was timbering. He told how the big beams called "headers" held up the roof, and single posts or a pile of "crib-blocks" held up the headers.

Tired of crawling now, Tina sat down to rest. It was so black inside the mine she could see nothing except the small circle of light from her lamp. In front of her the coal wall looked shiny, black and wet. She saw water running down. She turned her head to shine her light on Jeff, but he was not there.

"Jeff, where are you?" Tina asked in a whisper.

Jeff did not answer. There was not a sound. Tina listened carefully. Then she heard a roaring. It sounded like Grandma's pretty sea shell when she held it up to her ear. Was the inside of the earth like the sea? Tina heard water dripping —then a rustle—something was moving close by. She bent her head and the light shone down. What was it? A strange sound, a little squeak . . .

"A rat! A rat!" Tina cried.

She started to get up, bumped her head on the top and fell over in a puddle of water. The next minute Jeff and Uncle Jack came back and took her by the hand.

"What? Scared of a rat?" said Uncle Jack. "Why, the rat is the miner's best friend. Here's some left-over lunch in my bucket. Feed it to our little pets." He broke up some bread and scattered it.

"You call them *pets?*" said Tina. "It was as big as a cat. I saw it with my light."

Uncle Jack laughed. "The miners have been over-feeding that one!" he said. "Come now, let's go."

They crawled again, and at last were able to walk. When they came out into the sunshine, it blinded them. But oh, how good it was to see daylight again.

"Better not tell Mama you've been inside," said Uncle Jack. "It can be our secret. Mama might not like it. Women are funny that way."

Tina looked down at her clothes. She was black from head to foot. "What will Mama say when she sees me?"

"We still have to get her house coal," said Uncle Jack. "Getting coal is always dirty work."

The children laughed as they climbed back into Uncle Jack's car.

"Let's go up on the slate dump, Uncle Jack," said Jeff. "There's plenty of coal there."

"Hilda Krupa and her brother pick it up along the railroad tracks," said Tina. "Hilda says up at the tipple by the conveyor belt they get a lot when the mine's not working."

"Yes, and her brother steals it off the coal cars," said Jeff. "He could be arrested for that."

"Taking coal is stealing, like anything else," said Uncle Jack. "But if a man is out of work and has a big family like the Krupas and they need it to keep warm and to cook with, nobody says anything."

"But when they gather up coal to *sell* it, that's different," said Jeff.

"Willie Krupa came and tried to sell some to Mama yesterday," said Tina.

"That's O.K.," said Uncle Jack. "Old Man Krupa has leased a house-coal mine from Grandpa. Those big boys, Willie and Paul, can get it out with wheelbarrows and sell it. That will help the family out until the old man gets a job."

The car was winding its way up the side of Laurel Mountain. On one side of the road, the houses sat on high posts, with porches high above the road, overlooking the valley. On the other side, the roofs of houses were lower than the road, for the houses were built on a lower level. A banty hen with a flock of banty chicks crossed the road ahead. Men's bank clothes hung from clotheslines by the houses, blowing in the breeze. A long blacksnake lay dead in the grass at one side.

The road wound around until it came to the top of Slate Dump Hill. Uncle Jack stopped the car and the children climbed out.

"Oh, I just love to come here!" cried Tina, clapping her hands.

"Be careful and don't burn yourself," said Uncle Jack. "You don't see the fire except at night."

Coal cars on a high trestle track brought waste slate from Linden Number 3 mine and dumped it over the mountainside. Dumping had gone on for many, many years until the pile was almost as large as the mountain itself and the valley was filled with slate.

The new part of the dump was burning and giving off sulphur fumes. Whenever the weather was damp, the slate began to burn by spontaneous combustion. It burned better on rainy days, with smoke rolling up in clouds. Down at the bottom where the burned slate had cooled, it was red in color. Burned slate, called "red-dog" was sometimes used for road-building material.

"Don't go over there," called Tina, pointing to the railroad track and the new part. "The dump stinks bad over there."

"But where it's hot and burning," said Uncle Jack, "that's where we find the best coal. But we must be careful and not burn ourselves."

Uncle Jack was like a boy himself, always ready for fun. It had not been too many years since he too had roamed the slate dumps, like all coal camp children, and had fun on them.

"Let's pick up what coal we can," he said.

The children set to work, but soon Tina got tired. She stood still and looked about. She was high above the coal camp. She could see the railroad track and the creek and the tipple down in the valley. She could see the rows of houses up and down the slopes. She spotted the Wilson house on a corner. Was that Mama or Celia out in the yard hanging up clothes?

There was Grandpa's house too, not so far below her. The dump was so close, she seemed to be right on top of the house.

"Are they going to keep on dumping slate here forever and ever?" asked Tina.

"They could dump slate into this hollow for a hundred years and not half fill it," said Uncle Jack.

"But won't they cover Gramp's house up?" asked the girl.

"They don't dump on this side any more," said Uncle Jack. "They're dumping back in Crabapple Hollow now."

"Crabapple Hollow—that's where Uncle Chick lives," said Tina.

She picked up a piece of slate and threw it down the slope. Maybe she could hit Grandpa's chimney. Jeff began throwing too.

Uncle Jack laughed and said, "Trying to hit Grandpa on the head?"

"No," said Tina. "Just having fun."

"Maybe we could hit the ponies in the pasture," Jeff said.

"Don't you dare try it," said Tina.

"Hey! You kids aren't helping me much," said Uncle Jack. "Guess I'll go over to the Krupas' house-coal mine and get the tubs filled. That'll be quicker, since your mother's waiting for her coal. You kids want to stay here and play?"

Tina and Jeff nodded.

"Roll your sacks down the hill when they are full of coal and I'll stop and get them." Uncle Jack got in his car and rode off.

"Here come Trig and Dede," said Jeff, "and Virgil Tucker."

"Good! Now we'll have fun," said Tina.

Trig and Dede were cousins, Uncle Chick's children. They were a little older than Tina and Jeff. Trig was a small wiry boy, always daring. Dede had curly hair which Tina envied. Virgil lived just a block away from the Wilsons. They had come to Grandpa's and now they climbed up the dump from there. They had seen Jeff and Tina at the top.

Trig and Dede and Virgil kept on climbing, but sometimes the slate started sliding and took them down again. After a tumble, they had to get up and start all over. That made it all the more fun. At last they reached the top.

"Coal will bounce up and hit you," said Trig, "but slate just slides."

"The more you slide, the slicker it gets," said Virgil.

"I brought some cardboards," said Dede. "Let's slide down."

The children sat on the cardboards and started sliding. They slid down the slate dump and walked up again. Oh, what fun it was! Then they picked up pieces of slate and threw them. Each time they would race down to see if they could find the particular piece they had thrown.

Tina and Dede left the boys and started to look for red-dog stones. They loved the pretty colors in them. Tina stepped on a stone and cried out, "Red-dog stones are pretty but sharp!" She began to fill her pocket.

Then Dede stepped in a low place and sank down. She pulled pulled her foot out quickly. "Ouch! That's hot!" she called. "Oh—h—h! My leg's burned!"

Tina ran over. "Couldn't you see the smoke?"

"I thought it was just dew," said Dede, half-crying. "Gee! My leg hurts—it's burned."

Above her sock, her leg began to turn red. Tina helped her limp back up the dump where the boys were.

"What's the matter with you, Dede?" asked Trig.

"I burned my leg," said Dede. "That red-dog is hot!"

Trig looked at her leg. "Better go down and get Grandma to put some salve on it, before it blisters," he said.

Dede started off down the hill limping. She waved good-bye to Tina.

"Oh look!" cried Jeff. "I found a fossil."

Tina and Trig crowded close to see. The piece of slate was imprinted with lacy fern marks.

"I bet this piece is a million years old," said Jeff.

"Shucks!" said Trig. "I don't believe it." ·

"I found some petrified wood once," said Virgil.

After the sacks were filled with coal, Jeff tied them up and rolled them down to the bottom of the hill. The children walked back to the far side of the dump. Here young oak and birch trees had taken root in the barren slate and were trying to grow. A scared rabbit ran out, then disappeared in a hollow. Patches of grass were trying to grow—brown grass that never turned green.

"I know where there's an old mine," said Trig. "It's caved in and got bats in it."

"Where's it at?" asked Virgil.

"Up on Deerfoot Mountain, at the head of Crabapple Holler," said Trig. "The entry's high up in the bushes. You boys ever been there?"

"No," said Jeff.

"I know where it is," said Virgil.

"Want to go with me sometime?" asked Trig. "I'll show you where it is."

"Well—maybe," said Jeff. "But Uncle Jack says old mines are not safe."

"He's just afraid to go in one himself," said Trig. "I'm not."

Trig and Virgil started off towards home.

"Oh Jeff," said Tina, "let's go down to Gramp's pasture and ride the ponies."

"Not today," said Jeff. "We'd better go straight home or Mama will be out looking for us."

When Tina and Jeff got home, Mama said, "Uncle Jack brought the house coal hours ago. Where have you been?"

"We stayed up on the slate dump to play," said Tina. "Trig and Dede came and Dede burned her leg—not bad, though."

Mama took a good look at the girl.

"And what did *you* do, to get so black?" she asked. "You look like a coal miner!"

It was hard for Tina to keep a secret. Before she knew it, she had blurted out the truth.

"Uncle Jack told us not to tell you . . ." she added.

"Oh, that bad brother of mine," said Mama. "He's always up to something."

"I've been in the mine," said Tina. "I've been under this house, and all the way under Laurel Mountain. I've been under the dime store in Mapleton!"

"Oh no!" said Mama, laughing. "Little girls don't go into mines."

Jeff came in looking as black as his sister.

"Have you been in the mine, too?" asked Mama.

"Yep!" said Jeff. "Uncle Jack took us in. Gee! It's wonderful back in there. So black and spooky. Not hot and not cold. Good air to breathe."

"Grandma always said the air in the mine is good for whooping cough," said Mama. "But Uncle Jack didn't take you in the big mine, did he?"

"Oh yes," said Tina. "In Linden Number 3, Daddy's mine."

"Yes," said Jeff. "He had some work to do, so he took us in with him. We went in about a mile maybe and we saw the holes where the coal had been taken out, and the machinery and the timbering . . .”

“We wore hard-shell bank caps on our heads, with electric lights to see by,” said Tina.

Mama and Celia laughed. “Bet you looked pretty,” said Celia.

“Why didn't you take me?” asked Ronnie.

“Oh, you're too little,” said Tina.

“Well, I'm sure of one thing,” said Mama. “All kids raised in a coal camp must have guardian angels to take care of them, or they'd never survive!”

Chapter Three

PAYDAY

"BREAD, soup meat, a bag of pinto beans . . ." Mama made out a grocery list and handed Tina the old knit shopping bag.

Celia spoke up, "And a bottle of baby oil for Letty. Don't forget."

Tina started out the door.

"Here, take this," said Mama. "You wouldn't buy much with no money, if you didn't have Daddy's scrip card."

Tina took the scrip card in her hand and looked at it. At the top was the name of the company and the name of the mine—Linden Number 3. Next was Daddy's name, Walter

31

Wilson, and his check number, 521, and the name of the month and year stamped in blue. The card was divided into two columns for the two halves of the month, one dated from the first to the fifteenth, the other from the fifteenth to the thirtieth. At the bottom it said in small print, "This card must be brought or sent to the office when advances are desired."

"What are 'advances,' Mama?" asked Tina.

"That's the scrip we buy food with," said Mama. "The

company *advances* us the money before payday. You give the card to Mr. Frazier at the office window and ask him for a dollar and a half in scrip. That ought to be enough for today."

Mama sighed as she glanced at the card in the girl's hand. So many dates had amounts advanced marked beside them. Would there be anything left by the time payday came around?

"Seems as if we spend every penny Daddy earns before he gets it," she said.

"That's the truth!" said Celia. She turned to Tina. "Remember now, baby oil for Letty."

Tina went out the door and down the street. She felt very important to go to the company store alone. She wondered if she would see anyone she knew. Exciting things were happening along the way. The Murphys' cat was chasing a chicken. Mrs. Bryant was hanging clothes on her line. Dave Hurley, the little crippled boy, was hobbling on his crutches. His sisters, Barbara and Betty ran out to say hello. And there was Peggy Murphy fighting her brother again.

Tina wanted to stop but didn't. Clutching her scrip card and shopping bag, she walked on down to the corner.

"Tina! Christina Wilson!" a voice called behind her.

Tina looked back and there was Hilda Krupa. Hilda lived up on the hill by the slate dump. Now she came tearing down like a house afire. She stumbled once and nearly fell. Hilda liked to joke about her big feet. Hilda was a good friend and Tina liked her.

"You going to the store?" asked Hilda.

"Yes," said Tina, primly. "I have to do some shopping for my mother."

"You got *money?*" asked Hilda. "Real money?"

"No," admitted Tina. "I've got my daddy's scrip card."

"I'm going to the store, too," said Hilda.

"What for?" asked Tina.

"I have to tell Aunt Tillie something," said Hilda. She put her arm around Tina's waist. "Let's get ice cream cones," she said.

"I won't have scrip enough," said Tina.

"Candy then," said Hilda.

"No," said Tina, " 'cause my big sister needs baby oil for her baby and I'm not sure I'll have enough for that."

"Gum, then," said Hilda. "Just one pack."

"You ask your Aunt Tillie to get it for you," said Tina. "She works in the store."

"Oh, she never gives me anything," said Hilda.

The two girls walked on toward the company store, but when they came to the railroad track they had to wait.

A train whistle sounded and a train came puffing along the track. It was a long line of coal cars pulled by a steam engine. The engine huffed and puffed, as smoke and cinders fell.

The train was late today. It usually went by before the men came off the day shift. It went up to the coal-tipple with empties every day at noon, and came back with the coal cars filled with coal in different sizes, some in large lumps, some in small. It took the coal out of the valley where it had been mined.

"I wonder where that coal is going," said Tina.

"How should I know?" said Hilda.

"*I* know," said Tina. "It's going *all over the world!*"

"How do you know that?" asked Hilda.

"My daddy told me," said Tina. "He said that when he digs coal down under the ground, he's bringing electric lights and heat and all kinds of things to people all around the world!"

But Hilda had no imagination and was not listening.

"Let's run!" she cried. "I don't want to get cinders in my hair!"

The train went chugging on, scattering a shower of cinders through the valley. The company store was a large red brick two-storied building beside the railroad track. Across the front in large letters was a sign that said, MOUNTAIN VALLEY STORES.

The girls ran in at the big front door. It was cool and quiet inside, for there were only a few customers. Tina knew everybody who worked there. Mr. Frazier was in the office on one side, marking down rows of figures in a large ledger. Mr.

Diehl, the butcher, was sharpening knives. "Aunt Tillie"—
Hilda's aunt was showing a woman dry goods over her
counter. The Sonnenberg boy was putting canned goods on
a shelf.

Tina liked the company store. It was different from the
stores in Mapleton, the big town up on the hill. It had a special smell all its own, and it was always neat and clean. The
ceiling was as high as a church. The counters and aisles ran
from front to back. Everything was sold at the company
store—groceries, fuel, clothing, housewares, tools, meat, hard-
ware and furniture.

Hilda ran first to the candy counter, then to the dry goods
department where Aunt Tillie worked.

Tina went timidly to the barred window of the office and
peeped in. The counter inside and a large desk were filled
with papers and ledgers. Mr. Frazier was adding figures and
mumbling with his lips. He did not see or hear the little girl.
Tina stood first on one foot, then on the other. She stuck her
scrip card up through the bars. But Mr. Frazier did not even
know she was there.

Tina could not wait all day, so she coughed. It was only a
tiny cough, but it made Mr. Frazier jump. He made a blot
on the page of his big book, picked up a blotter and blotted
it. He came to the window and his piercing black eyes rested
on the girl who stood outside it. He reached for her scrip
card.

"What's your name?" he asked.

"Christina Wilson," said Tina.

"How much?" he asked.

"A dollar and a half," said Tina meekly.

Mr. Frazier counted it out in scrip and handed the coins to her.

Tina looked at them in her hand. They were almost like real money, but when you wanted to spend them at the stores in town, they weren't worth as much as money. They were

just a substitute for money. Some of the coins looked like silver and some like brass, but they weren't real silver or brass. They all had the name of the Mountain Valley Coal Company on them, and the words, "Payable in Merchandise Only." Each coin had a hole stamped in the middle, shaped like a number, a two or a three.

"The pennies are larger than the nickels," Tina said as she counted. She had two half dollars, a quarter, two nickels, a dime and five pennies.

"How much did you get?" Hilda came and peeked over her shoulder.

Tina closed her hand and wouldn't show her. She went to the grocery counter and bought her bread and beans. Then she went to the meat counter for her soup meat. Mr. Diehl was very slow, but finally he got it ready for her. She had enough left for the baby oil at the drug counter.

Tina put each thing in her shopping bag. She had just one nickel left over. Quickly she tucked it into her shoe, so Hilda would not see it.

"Let's get candy," begged Hilda.

Tina shook her head.

"Why doesn't your Aunt Tillie buy you candy?" she asked. "She works here."

"I asked her," said Hilda. "She says they don't give her any candy free."

"Well, then . . ." said Tina.

Hilda took Tina over to the dry goods counter. Aunt Tillie was a middle-aged woman with glasses on her nose. She nodded to Tina, but not a word was said about candy. Aunt Tillie looked at Tina's shopping bag.

"You shopping for your mama?" she asked. "You find everything you need? Can I sell you some of this pretty red plaid for a nice warm dress for winter?" She held a piece up high and let it fall in even folds.

"No," said Tina. "Mama says everything's too high here. When we got *money,* we go to town. Things are cheaper there."

Aunt Tillie tossed her head.

"Here at the company store we sell only *good* merchandise," she said. "For cheap stuff, yes—you can go to town."

Hilda looked at Tina.

"Here you can buy what you want with *scrip,*" said Hilda. "Before payday even!"

"That's just the trouble," said Tina. "Mama says our money's all gone before we ever see it. Besides, when they're out of something here at the company store, they make you wait too long before they get it."

Aunt Tillie turned her back. Because she worked there, she was always loyal to the company store.

As the children left, Hilda said to Tina, "You shouldn't say those things to my Aunt Tillie. She don't like it."

"But it's true and you know it," said Tina.

"I suppose it is," said Hilda. As they walked along, Hilda begged Tina to go home with her.

"I'll go as far as my grandma's," said Tina. "I want to see Snowball and that new pony called Bright Eyes. But I can't stay long because Mama is waiting."

The girls turned off on a side street and started up the hill. They passed the Collins house where a lot of flowers were blooming. A row of tall sunflowers grew by the fence. Dahlias were in bloom by the gate.

Soon they came to Hilda's house, Number 214. It was on the highest road, skirting the mountain, not far from the slate dump. Behind Hilda's house rose a black mountain of slate, higher than the mountain itself.

"Let's go up to the top and slide down," said Hilda. "Over on the other side, where my mom won't see us."

"Some other time," said Tina. "I have to hurry back. As soon as I see the ponies, I'll go on home."

"All right for you," said Hilda. "I'll be mad at you!"

Tina smiled. She knew Hilda never stayed mad very long. Hilda went in her back door. She turned and called back, "See you in school tomorrow."

But when Tina got to Grandma's, she couldn't get away as soon as she expected to, for exciting things were going on. Grandma and Aunt Effie, Uncle Chick's wife, and Mrs. Tucker, Virgil's mother, were out in the yard making apple butter. Grandpa was there too, sitting on his straight-backed chair, stirring the seething sauce in the big twenty gallon copper kettle.

"See my 'stirrer'?" he asked, lifting his wooden paddle. "It's called a 'horse's head!'"

Tina laughed. The queer-shaped board at the end of the broom handle did look like a skinny horse head. At one end it was rounded to scrape the bottom of the kettle, and it had holes bored in it to let the sauce run through.

Grandpa's chin was white with unshaved whiskers, and his

eyes, under the visor of his cap, were blue and merry. Tina looked into the bubbling, simmering red sauce.

"Gramp, want me to stir a turn?" she asked.

"Sure." Grandpa offered her the handle.

"Oh, it's popping!" cried Tina. "I don't want to get burned!"

"Don't be afraid, Christina. Take it," said Grandpa. "I've got to put more wood on the fire."

The kettle set on a low wall of bricks, daubed with clay to keep the flames inside.

"Now don't you make it too hot, Gramp," called Grandma, who was resting in the shade.

Tina put her shopping bag on the ground and began to move the "stirrer" back and forth.

"Where are those new ponies, Gramp?" she asked.

"Can't fool with ponies today," said Grandpa. "Got to git this apple butter made." He pushed some sticks of wood under the kettle.

"What a job!" Grandma mopped her face. "Effie and I peeled apples all day yesterday, and I started the sass at six this morning. Looks like it'll be night before I git it canned."

"How much sugar did it take?" asked Mrs. Tucker.

"Thirty pounds," said Grandma. "I figger it'll make ten gallons. It's got about two more hours to go, before it glazes over."

Grandma was a round plump woman, with her gray hair

in a braided ring at the back of her head. She looked much like Tina's mother, but was stouter.

Tina soon got tired of stirring.

"I got to go," she said. "Mama don't know where I am."

Aunt Effie said, "Guess it's my turn with that stirrer." She got up and told Tina to go. Tina picked up her shopping bag.

"Hey!" called Grandpa. "You can't go without seeing the ponies!"

Grandpa took Tina's hand and they walked to the barn. He opened the door, and there stood the two new ponies, Bright Eyes and Diamond. Tina looked them over.

"Why, Bright Eyes has eyes as blue as the sky!" she said. "And Diamond—he must be a black diamond. His fur is black like a bear's."

Grandpa laughed. "He's a bad one. We'll have trouble breaking him."

"Can I have a ride, Gramp?" asked Tina.

Grandpa brought Bright Eyes out of the barn. He put the bridle on her and helped the girl up. He walked beside the pony, leading him. They went up and down the lane.

"Oh, Gramp!" said Tina. "He's better than Snowball. He rides as smooth as a rocking chair!"

Grandpa laughed and went back in the barn.

Tina patted Bright Eyes and talked to him. The pony started to turn around and nip at the girl. Then he tried to throw her off.

"Oh, Bright Eyes, *don't!*" cried Tina.

Grandpa hurried out.

"He's trying to *bite* me!" said Tina.

"With a new pony, you have to be careful," said Grandpa, "until you get to know him and he gets used to you. Don't ride him too much at first. Better get off."

"I like Bright Eyes," said Tina. "Can't I have a pony all my own, Gramp?"

Grandpa shook his head.

"Ponies are not playthings, they cost a lot of money," he said. "You'd better run along home now, or your mama will think you're lost."

Tina said goodbye and hurried home as fast as she could go.

Payday was always exciting, because it meant shopping. Payday came every two weeks on "the first day of the half," that is, on the first and fifteenth of each month.

"The children need school clothes," said Mama. "I'll get a winter coat for Tina and Jeff a warm jacket. All three of them need shoes."

Early in the morning, Mama and the children left the house. The whole valley was filled with fog and they had to walk slowly. The air was heavy with black smelly coal smoke. When they got to the company store, cars were already parked and people were lined up in front waiting to get in when the door opened. Men were waiting to be paid off, and a few women and children waited to collect their daddies' pay.

Mrs. Wilson spoke to Mr. Murphy and Mr. Hurley, her neighbors. Then Mrs. Bryant came up to talk.

"It feels like overcoat weather, don't it?" said Mama.

"Snow will be flying soon," said Mrs. Bryant. "Got your winter coal in yet?"

"Part of it," said Mama. "Jack promised to bring the rest this week. Our heater's still out on the back porch where it's been all summer. We must bring it in soon."

"I'm trying to get all my bedding washed up before cold weather comes," said Mrs. Bryant. "Done your winter shopping yet?"

"No," said Mama. "I thought I'd try to get some school clothes for the kids today."

Ronnie spoke up. "I want new shoes, Mama."

Up ahead, the store door opened and the line began to move.

"That is, if there's any money left," said Mama.

"You said it," added Mrs. Bryant. "Real money's as scarce as hen's teeth."

At last it was Mama's turn at the office window. She handed in Daddy's statement, which showed the number of hours he had worked during the "half" and the amount he had earned. Mr. Frazier handed her Daddy's pay in a small brown envelope, on which were marked the various amounts held back.

Mama looked at it and frowned: Union dues, doctor bills, insurance, rent, water and extras. She turned to Mrs. Bryant and said, "Even saving the bathhouse fee doesn't help much. The kids need school clothes even if we go in debt for them . . . Some day, I hope we can get caught up."

Mrs. Bryant nodded in sympathy.

Tina looked up at Mama and said, "I like scrip. Don't you?"

Mama and Mrs. Bryant laughed.

"I don't know what we'd do without it," Mama said.

Then they went to the clothing department. Mama looked at a warm coat for Tina, but when she heard the price, she shook her head. Jeff was the only one who got what he needed, a warm plaid jacket. Mama said Tina's and Ronnie's old coats would do for another winter.

"I want new shoes," said Ronnie. "My soles are all worn out."

But Mama closed her purse. "No shoes today," she said. "We'll wait till the next half for shoes." Mama picked out her groceries and they all went home.

One day when Tina got home from school, Daddy was already there, sitting in the porch swing with his feet up on the railing. Tina sat down beside him and told him all about her nice teacher, Miss Sanford. Soon they heard a whining noise. The door was open and they could hear Mama and Celia talking inside.

"Is that the baby crying?" asked Mama.

"No," said Celia, "she's sound asleep. She hasn't stirred since I put her down."

"It's that dog whining then," said Mama. "Where's Queenie? Under the house?"

"Sounds like it," said Celia.

Mama sent Tina out to quiet the dog. But when Tina returned, the dog howled again.

"It worries me," said Mama. "Everytime Queenie howls, somebody gets sick or hurt."

"Don't you go to borrowing trouble," called Daddy from the porch. "Here I am safe and sound. You've got no call to worry."

Tina put her arm around Daddy's shoulder. She hoped nothing would happen to him.

"Remember last year when you lost those two fingers?" said Mama. "Queenie howled then too, so I knew something was wrong."

When Jeff came in, Mama told him to look the dog over, to see if she was hurt in any way.

"Nothing wrong with Queenie," said Jeff, "unless she's got the stomachache."

Even Mama laughed.

"Dogs don't get stomachache," said Tina.

"I bet they do if they've been poisoned," said Jeff.

"Don't be foolish!" called Daddy. "Queenie hasn't had poison."

"Maybe it's Jack then," said Mama.

"Jack doesn't get stomachache either," said Daddy. They all laughed.

Mama came to the door. "Walter, do you think something's happened to Jack?" she asked seriously.

"Don't be silly, Mary Kate," said Daddy. "Jack's safer down in the mine than up on the highway, driving his car at seventy miles an hour. Jack's worked fifteen years in the mine and never been hurt yet."

Mama went back to the kitchen.

"Why does she worry so about Uncle Jack?" asked Tina.

"Just because he's her baby brother, she keeps fussing over him," said Daddy.

But just the same, Mama was uneasy.

"He's settin' crib-blocks pretty far in, he told me," said Mama. "That's dangerous work. That slate can fall if you look at it." The dog howled again. "Queenie senses things," Mama went on. "That dog knows when somebody's in danger. Oh, if it's Jack . . ."

Nighttime came and the family went to bed. The dog was restless under the house and howled at intervals. Tina could not sleep. She had heard many stories of mine injuries and disasters that happened to other people. Was it the Wilsons turn now? Was something bad going to happen? Her mother's fears had been passed on to the little girl.

She slept awhile, then a sound woke her again. What was it? Was Mama up already, "loading" Daddy's bucket in the kitchen? It was still dark. The mine whistle always blew in the morning while Tina was still in bed, and Daddy always went off down the hill before it was light. She hadn't heard the whistle. Wasn't it time yet?

Suddenly Tina heard a tapping at the window. Then she heard voices and knew Daddy was up. Daddy was talking to someone. Tina listened and barely caught the words, "Jack is under the slate."

"Under the slate"—even the youngest coal camp child knew what that meant. A block of slate had fallen from the roof of the mine, and Uncle Jack was under it . . . Beloved Uncle Jack, Mama's "baby brother." Uncle Jack, the children's best friend. Tina's heart skipped a beat. Was he dead?

It was quiet now. The man—it sounded like Uncle Chick —had gone away. Daddy was moving around, putting on his clothes. Then she heard Mama.

"Where are you going, Walter? Is anything wrong?"

Had Mama heard the tap on the window and the man's message?

"Somebody came," said Mama. "Who was it?"

The dog howled again.

"It was Chick," Mama said. "What did he come for? Oh, I know. Somebody's hurt—it's *Jack!*"

Then Tina heard Daddy's stern voice, "The mine is no place for a woman to be, when a man is hurt."

Tina heard Mama crying and she burst into tears herself. Daddy went out and the sound of his footsteps died quickly away. Tina tiptoed into Mama's bedroom and crept into her bed. She put her arms around Mama and they cried together.

It seemed a long time before Daddy got back. Mama and the children were all up and dressed. The first pink streaks of daylight flooded the sky over the mountain. Mama's face was set and white, as she met Daddy at the door.

"Is he dead?" she asked.

"No." Daddy put his arms around Mama and held her tight.

"I told you not to borrow trouble," he said. "The roof was bad and Jack was setting up crib-blocks like you said. A big piece of slate came down and crushed his shoulder and arm. He jumped out of the way just in time to escape the worst of it. They had to take him to the hospital to find out how bad it was. His collarbone is broken and some bones in his arm . . ."

"Just his arm?" said Mama. "Oh, thank God!"

"It would have broken his back," said Daddy, "if he hadn't stepped to one side."

"Poor Jack!" said Mama. "A broken arm."

"How long will he have to stay in the hospital?" asked Jeff.

"I don't know," said Daddy. "His shoulder is crushed and will be put in a cast until the bones heal."

"Poor Jack!" said Mama. "He's never been sick in bed for a single day in all his life. How can he stand it?"

"*Lucky* Jack, you'd better say," said Daddy. "He's lucky he's still alive, and he's lucky his back's not broken."

"I'm glad it was only his arm," said Celia.

"So am I," said Ronnie.

"I'll take him some of Grandma's flowers," said Tina.

Jeff called Queenie and went out the door without saying a word.

Chapter Four

HARDSHIP

"How's Jack? Is he hurt bad?"

Before Tina left for school, the neighbors began to come in. Although the Wilsons had no telephone, the news of Jack's injury had spread. Mrs. Bryant came back and forth with messages from people who had phoned at her house to inquire.

Others came to the door. Celia met them with baby Letty on her arm. She told them all she knew. Then Uncle Chick and Grandma came in Uncle Jack's car to take Celia and Mama and Daddy to the hospital. Mama hustled Jeff and

Tina off to school. When she got there, school had begun.

Tina could not keep her mind on her lessons at all. She kept looking out of the window. The schoolhouse was on Blackberry Hill and across the valley she could see the coal-tipple—the big black ugly thing standing there by Linden Number 3, where they brought Uncle Jack out on a stretcher, crushed and hurt. Tina put her head down on her desk and began to cry again.

A kind hand touched her shoulder.

"What's the matter, Christina?" asked Miss Sanford.

"It's Uncle Jack . . ." began Tina.

"Jack! Jack Ferris!" cried Miss Sanford, frightened. "Has anything happened to Jack?"

"He's hurt bad," said Tina. "They took him to the hospital last night."

"Oh *no!*" cried Miss Sanford. Tears came to her eyes, but she brushed them away. "I'm sure you don't feel like studying much today, Tina. Wouldn't you like to go home?"

"Now?" asked Tina. "Before school is out?"

"Yes," said Miss Sanford.

"Nobody's there," said Tina. "They've all gone to the hospital."

"Is there any other place you'd like to go?"

"Grandma Ferris's," said Tina. "But she's gone to the hospital too. Uncle Jack is her baby boy."

"Is your grandpa at home?" asked Miss Sanford.

"I suppose so," said Tina. "He wasn't in the car."

"You go and see Grandpa," said the teacher. "He has some mine ponies, hasn't he?"

"Yes, two new ones," said Tina.

The thought of the mine ponies cheered Tina up. How was Snowball? Was her hurt foot well and had she gone back to work? And those two new ponies with the pretty names—Bright Eyes and Diamond. She had almost forgotten them. It would be nice to see the ponies again.

But when she got to Grandpa's, her happiness faded.

The house was closed and empty. Tina hurried to the

barn as fast as she could. Was something wrong here too? Grandpa was in one of the stalls, doing something. She heard him muttering to himself.

Tina came in and called out, "Can I have a pony ride, Gramp?"

"Pony ride!" growled Grandpa. "What's the matter? Are you crazy, girl? All you can think of is pony rides. When are you going to get a little sense?"

Tina's heart sank. Grandpa was cross today. His rheumatism must be bad. That always made him cross. He came out of the stall limping. Yes—that meant a bad knee.

Tina looked in and saw a sad sight. The white pony, Snowball, was lying down and foam was coming from her mouth. She must be very sick. Grandpa was putting a brown liquid into a bottle with a long neck. He paid no attention to Tina at all.

"What's the matter with Snowball?" asked Tina.

"Matter enough!" said Grandpa. "Bad case of colic. Can't hardly walk, can't stand up—just lays around."

" 'Colic.' What's that?" asked Tina.

"Don't *you* know?" Grandpa's eyes pierced hers. "It's good old-fashioned tummy ache, same as you kids get from eatin' green apples. That fool pony broke down her fence and got over to that apple tree and ate herself sick. She's got a bad case of cramps."

"Like Jeff had that time?" Tina asked.

"Yep! Same thing," said Grandpa. "Had to have the vet come and give her some dope or she'd a died."

Grandpa took the bottle in the stall and got ready to give the pony another dose.

"Come here, Christina! You hold her head up," said Grandpa, "so I can pour it down her throat."

Tina never knew how she did it, but together she and Grandpa got the medicine down. Snowball opened one eye and looked up as if she knew they were trying to help her.

"Snowball can't have apples any more," said Grandpa. "You kids must remember that. Another case of colic will finish her sure."

"We don't want Snowball to die, do we?" asked Tina.

"Not on your life," said Grandpa.

The pony seemed to be resting easier, so Grandpa and Tina walked out to the pasture gate. There were three other ponies there besides Bright Eyes and Diamond. The others were Stubby, Red and Spot. Grandpa rented them out to other punch mines.

"You tell Jeff to come and ride them," said Grandpa. "If they get too fat, they won't work. Tell him to come by each evening and give them a run. They need more exercise."

Grandpa and Tina looked at the new ponies and talked about how pretty they were. Tina almost forgot about Uncle Jack. Then they went back to the house. Grandpa stopped in the kitchen and brought out a dish of Grandma's freshly made cookies. Tina and Grandpa helped themselves and sat down in the porch swing to visit.

This was Grandpa's favorite place, for he could see the coal camp which he loved and where he had lived all his life. He could see the black tipple, symbol of his life-work in the mine. Grandpa liked to sit there to dream and remember his past life. As he talked to the little girl, he seemed almost to be talking to himself.

"I've been a miner for sixty years," said Grandpa. "Began when I was ten years old because my daddy was a miner before me. Miners are clean people, honest people. There's lots of hardship and long hours, but I never had an accident till

I'd worked fifty-nine years, then I lost one finger. I retired at sixty and got my pension. Then I started in business for myself—leasing pony mines. I can't give up and do nothing. It's bad for a man to give up and quit."

What he said made Tina think of Uncle Jack again.

"Gramp," said Tina, "do you think Uncle Jack's going to die?"

Grandpa turned to her quickly. "Die, nothing!" he said. "It would take more than a ton of slate to kill that scalawag! Broken shoulder and collarbone—what's that? Nothing!"

Grandpa reached out and took Tina's hand in his own. He rocked the swing gently back and forth, humming a little tune. Tina felt better as he told her tales of things Uncle Jack used to do when he was a little boy. "Run along home now," he added. "Your mama'll be looking for you. And don't you worry about Uncle Jack."

The days were getting short now with cooler weather, and the sky was dark with clouds. It was foggy in the valley, and as Tina ran down the hill, she saw the fog coming up to meet her. A dense white fog was rising from the coal camp, blotting out the houses. Tina ran fast until it reached her, then she had to slow up.

Suddenly she was in the middle of it. She could hardly see the houses now. A light went on in one house—whose was it? The road turned and she stepped in a ditch. She could not tell which way she was going. She wanted to get home before the fog got bad. All the houses looked alike. Even in broad daylight, Tina had to count them to find which one she lived in. Now she could not see the numbers on them at all. How would she ever find her house in the fog?

She kept bravely on. Now there was a fence by the road. She kept her hand on it, walking in the grass. A truck zoomed out of nowhere. She heard but could not see it, until the dim lights were almost on her. Then it went on. Which way was the road? There were no sidewalks—she'd better keep hold of the fence. When the fence ended, she came to a ditch. Jumping across, she was afraid she was in the road again. What if a car—a big truck filled with coal, should come along before she saw it?

Tina tried to hold back the tears, but couldn't. She stumbled on, not knowing where she was going. Then she found another fence with pickets. She felt the pickets one by one, until she came to the gate.

"I'll go in," she said. "I'll go in the house and see who lives here. I'll find out whose house it is."

The houses stood close to the road, the narrow porches in front. Tina went in the gate and found her way to the porch. Where were the lights? Where were the windows? Who lived here, anyway?

She came to the front door, which was shut tight. She knocked, but no answer came. She felt her way to the window at one side, and her heart sank, for it was boarded up.

She went back to the window on the other side of the door. It was boarded up too.

It was one of the empty houses. Nobody lived there. The family had gone away to some other town, where the father could get work. More and more families were leaving Linden. Tina tried to think whose house it could be, but the names of the families who had gone escaped her.

The house was empty, she could not go in. The fog was heavier now than ever. She looked down and could hardly see the front step. There was nothing to do but wait, so she sat down and leaned her head against the post. She folded her arms tightly together. The fog was so damp, it chilled her through and through. But at least, here she was safe.

Tina never knew how long she sat there. She must have dozed a while. Suddenly she woke up—a dog was barking. Was it Queenie, Jeff's own Queenie? She heard a boy's voice calling the dog, and there was Jeff as big as life. And the fog was gone. It had lifted to the mountain top and left the valley clear.

"So *there* you are!" Jeff said. "I've been hunting high and low for you."

"The fog . . . the fog . . ." began Tina.

"I went up to Gramp's and Gramp said you left there a long time ago," said Jeff. "When I got home, you hadn't come. So I went out to look for you."

"I got all turned around," said Tina. "I didn't know where

I was going. Whose house is this, anyhow?"

"Don't you even know where you are?" asked Jeff. "This is where the Davises used to live, right next to the Hurleys. You were almost home and didn't know it."

"I was afraid I'd be run over," said Tina. "A big coal truck came along and nearly hit me."

"You were smart to go up on a porch and wait," said Jeff. "That was the safest thing to do. Do you know what happened to that coal truck? It ran into the Murphys' fence, turned over and dumped all the coal in the Murphys' yard! They got a big load of coal for nothing!"

"Was the man hurt?" asked Tina.

"No, he jumped out," said Jeff. "But boy, was he scared! Come on home now and get warm. Daddy and I brought the coal heater in from the porch and set it up in the living room. Mama's got a nice warm fire going."

"Did they get back from the hospital?" asked Tina.

"Yes, they came back early," said Jeff.

"How's Uncle Jack?" asked Tina.

"Better," said Jeff. "Come on, let's run. I've got to get coal in. Here Queenie!"

The fog had lifted now. The children ran home and Tina felt warmer when she got there. But she went straight to the stove in the front room and held out her hands.

Waves of comforting heat radiated from the stove and filled the room. Daddy and Celia and baby Letty were sitting up close. They all loved the genial warmth of the coal heater. They talked cheerfully about Uncle Jack now, until Mama called them into the kitchen for supper.

When payday came again, Daddy was not at home. He had gone with Uncle Chick to Virginia to see about getting some mine equipment.

So Mama sent Jeff to the company store to draw Daddy's pay. Jeff put the statement in an inside pocket of his jacket, where it would be safe. Mama told Tina to go along with him, so she put on her old winter coat and tied a scarf over her head.

The day was cold for November and a stiff wind was blowing. The children started early, because they wanted to be
there when the office window opened.

They passed the Bryant house and saw Mrs. Bryant going
for water at the spigot in the Murphys' yard. Dave Hurley
on his crutches waved from his front porch. The next house
was the Davises' empty one, and then came the Murphys'. At
the gate stood Peggy. She was older than Tina and not very
friendly. She liked to pull Tina's hair and slap her on the
back. Sometimes it hurt.

"Where you kids goin'?" demanded Peggy.

"Down to the store," said Tina.

"Don't speak to her," whispered Jeff. "Don't tell her what
I'm going for."

"What are you going to the store on payday for?" asked
Peggy.

Neither Tina nor Jeff answered. They hurried on.

Peggy Murphy came running behind them.

"Bet I know what you're doin'," shouted Peggy. "Bet
you're gonna draw your daddy's pay!"

The children ran and did not answer. At the company
store, the line of men and a few women was already waiting.
Jeff and Tina took their places behind Mrs. Watkins, a large
stout woman. They saw Peggy Murphy lying in wait for
them. They saw Hilda Krupa come up and talk to Peggy.
They saw Cliff Crouse and Sammy Blagg come up on bicy-

cles. Peggy talked to them too, and pointed to Jeff and Tina.

Jeff felt worried, but did not tell Tina how he felt.

At last the window opened, and soon his turn came. There was over a hundred dollars for Daddy this time, even after various items had been charged out. Mr. Frazier smiled at Tina this time and told Jeff to button the envelope up tight, so he would not lose it. They walked slowly out the door side by side.

"You stay right by me, Tina," said Jeff, "no matter what happens."

"All right, Jeff," said Tina. "Here they come."

Sammy Blagg was a big boy and known to be a bully. Cliff Crouse was smaller, but liked to do whatever Sammy did. The boys left their bicycles beside the store and came over to Jeff. Jeff wished that Virgil Tucker were there. Together they could beat the two other boys up.

"This is a hold-up!" said Sammy. He pointed his fingers like a gun. "Hand it over."

Jeff smiled. "You're kiddin', Sammy. Do you think you're in a movie?"

Cliff Crouse said, "We need some cash. Hand us over a ten dollar bill."

Jeff turned to Tina and said, "Let's run."

The two ducked and started running, only to be blocked by Peggy Murphy and Hilda Krupa. "Give us what you got!" said Peggy.

"Why Hilda," said Tina. "I thought you were a friend of mine and not Peggy's."

There was no time for talk. Jeff and Tina ran as fast as they could go. Jeff cut across the railroad track and several yards, with Tina at his heels. Sammy and Cliff ran to get their bicycles and followed along the road, hoping to cut him off.

Tina ran as hard as she could, but could not keep up. There were Jeff's flying legs a mile ahead of her. She was

panting for breath, when a hard blow came on her shoulder. She fell to the ground with Peggy Murphy on top of her. She fought with her fists and kicked with her feet, but could not get Peggy off. Then a blow hit her in the face. Her nose began to bleed and she could not see out of her eye. She lay stunned for a moment.

Where was Jeff? Had he got away? Were they beating him up? Were they taking Daddy's pay? Tina felt like an old, old woman as she tried to get to her feet. Expecting more blows, she did not know which way to turn.

"Fighting again! All you coal camp kids do is fight!"

A woman leaned her head out of a window and shouted. "Go away, you bad little girl! Don't you ever come in my yard again! Fighting like a wild-cat! I'll call the police! Go away!"

Tina stumbled to her feet and tried to go on. Then she looked around to see if she was alone. Peggy Murphy was gone. She had done her worst and fled. But there stood Hilda Krupa, scared and white. Hilda's tears were rolling down her face. She came slowly over to Tina.

"Go away," said Tina. "I thought you were my friend."

"I *am!*" said Hilda, crying again. "I tried and tried to get Peggy Murphy to stop, but she wouldn't. I wasn't helping her, I was trying to make her stop. But she said she was going to give you a black eye . . . and she did." Hilda put her arm around Tina's shoulder.

"Peggy Murphy told me she hated you because your daddy's got work in the mine and her daddy's laid off," said Hilda. "So she wanted to get even with you."

"They were after my daddy's pay," said Tina, "those bad boys. Peggy put them up to it."

"They didn't get it," said Hilda. "Jeff got away, I saw him."

"How?" asked Tina.

"Virgil Tucker saw him running and called to him," said Hilda. "He jumped on a coal truck that was going to the tipple. Mr. Tucker, Virgil's daddy, was driving it. He stopped and Jeff got in the cab with him and Virgil."

"Oh, I'm glad," said Tina, wiping her bloody nose on her skirt. "I can't see much out of my eye. Do I look terrible?"

"Your eye's all swollen up," said Hilda.

Tina tried to brush off her clothes. "I'm covered with blood and mud. What will Mama say?"

"I'll tell her you couldn't help it," said Hilda.

"If you come home with me, Mama won't scold," said Tina.

Tina walked slowly home, with Hilda's arm around her waist. She hoped she would never see Peggy Murphy again. She dreaded going in the house. But it wasn't so bad, after all.

"Oh, those Murphys!" cried Mama. She listened to Hilda's story, then she bathed Tina's face, gave her a pad for her bloody nose and bandaged her eye. She had her change her soiled dress.

Jeff had already come home with Daddy's pay safe in his pocket. When Daddy came home and heard the tale he said, "So the kids still scrap at Scrappers Corners! That place has always had a bad name. When I was a boy, after the men were paid off, they'd get drunk and fight. The boys fought too—some carried knives and razors. I've got two or three holes in the back of my head made by rocks."

"What a week this has been!" said Mama. "Uncle Jack under the slate with a crushed shoulder and arm, Tina lost in the fog, Jeff chased by a bunch of hoodlums, Tina beaten up by a neighbor girl, Snowball sick with the colic . . . What next, I wonder?"

Although Mama did not realize it, worse was still to come and soon. The first day the next week, Daddy came home, tired and dejected. When Tina and Ronnie ran to meet him and look for a treat in his bucket, there was nothing there. He had not even a smile for them. He did not take them by the hand. The children knew something was wrong.

"What is it, Walter?" asked Mama at the supper table. "What are you worrying about? Uncle Jack is coming along fine, we've been able to pay something on his hospital bill, Tina's black eye is healing and she'll soon be pretty again, Snowball has recovered from the colic and can go back to work . . ."

"But I've lost my job!" said Daddy, laying down his fork.

"No!" said Mama. "Oh no! They can't do that to you, after all the years you've worked for them!"

"But they have," said Daddy. "They laid off twenty more men, and I'm one of the twenty."

"I can't believe it," said Mama slowly. "Somehow when things like this happen to other people, you can't believe it could ever happen to you . . ."

"Until it does," said Daddy. "Then you've got to believe it, whether you want to or not."

"Oh Daddy," said Tina. "You won't be a miner any more?"

"Sugar," said Daddy, "I'll be a miner till the day I die!"

Chapter Five

PONY

"JEFF! Get up! Jeff! Jeff!"

The boy felt someone shaking him, but he turned over and fell asleep again.

"JEFF! JEFF! How many times must I call you?"

Jeff opened his eyes and threw the covers back. It was time to get up and make the fire in the kitchen stove. He shivered as he pulled on his clothes. The room was very cold.

Jeff pulled up the blind and looked out.

The first snow was already on the ground. Its fresh whiteness made the dingy mine houses look still darker. Winter was early this year. Jeff hoped for lots of snow. Snow meant sliding and there were steep mountain slopes on all sides for that.

Jeff went in the kitchen where it was still colder. He opened the lids of the cook stove, put paper in and wood on top. He poured in a few drops of kerosene and lighted it. As soon as the wood began to burn, he put coal on.

The coal bucket was nearly empty. He had forgotten to fill it the night before. He unlocked the back door, took it

out and ran to the coal shed by the road. He shoveled coal in and brought it back.

Now Mama was up, getting breakfast. Oatmeal was cooking on the stove and Mama was mixing biscuits. The smell of coffee filled the air. Celia came out with baby Letty on her arm.

"Jeff," said Mama, "Uncle Chick left word for you to ride the new ponies over to the mine this morning. Go on up to Gramp's and get them. Uncle Chick's miners will be waiting for them."

"Tina!" called Jeff. "Come on. We have to take the ponies to the mine."

Tina came in the kitchen buttoning up her coat. The children ate quickly and went out. They ran up the hill to Grandpa's.

Jeff loved to ride the ponies to Uncle Chick's mine. He took them down on Monday mornings and brought them back on Friday nights. Sometimes Tina went along. This morning it was clammy and cold in the valley, for the sun had not yet peeped over the mountain.

Bright Eyes and Diamond, the new ponies, were working now. Okey Travis, the pony-driver, had been breaking them in for several weeks. Diamond was still a little wild. Each time Jeff got on, Diamond rared up and tried to throw him. But Jeff knew what to do.

"Go easy," called Grandpa. "Talk to him easy and he'll do what you say."

Diamond quieted down and Jeff rode on ahead. Tina followed on Bright Eyes. The children rode from Grandpa's pasture on around Laurel Mountain, until they came to a stripped section. Soil and rock on the side of the hill had been stripped off by bulldozers, exposing a huge cliff some forty feet high. Here was Uncle Chick's pony mine. At the bottom of the cliff was an entry with an "apron" of timbers over it. In front was a rickety tipple with a truck standing under it. Tracks led from the entry up the slope to the top of the tipple. Over on the right side was the fan entry.

A crude pony barn with a small fenced-off lot was at one side. In a low place, a pool of water had collected for the ponies to drink. The old ponies, Snowball and Ginger, had just come out of the mine with a load of coal. Okey Travis was unhitching them.

Snowball had recovered from her colic and was working again. Tina stared at the pony—she hardly knew her. Snowball's white fuzzy fur was black and dirty now from mud and coal dust. She called her name, but the pony did not turn her head. Snowball was not a pet any more. She had turned into a mine pony again. Did Snowball live two separate lives, and forget one while she was living the other?

Tina turned away. "I like Bright Eyes better, anyhow," she tried to comfort herself. "But now Bright Eyes will turn into a mine pony too . . ." Tears came to the girl's eyes.

Jeff and Tina watched Okey hitch Bright Eyes and Diamond to the coal car. Diamond was the leader, and Bright Eyes came behind. Okey put a miner's lamp on Diamond's forehead and hung the battery in a leather case from the pony's collar.

"Hup!" called Okey, snapping his strap in the air.

Okey slapped a board down on the coal car, called it his "saddle" and sat on it. The ponies went down the track at a run. At the entry, Okey had to duck his head and bend over, because it was so low. The roof of the mine just cleared the ponies' heads. In fact, Diamond had a leather shield on his forehead, so he would not be hurt if he hit any of the cross timbers. Uncle Chick's five miners were inside the mine, shoveling coal by hand into coal cars.

Jeff and Tina sat down and waited. Poor Bright Eyes! He would have to work hard now. And Diamond was flighty. Would he ever make a good mine pony? Tina hated to see the ponies start to work. They would not stay plump and round now. They would soon grow strong and muscular. They would get lean and lanky, and wouldn't be pretty any more.

When Uncle Chick came out, Jeff said, "Don't let Okey whip Diamond, Uncle Chick, or he'll have trouble."

"I know," said Uncle Chick. "If Diamond don't break, I'll have to sell him off and get another pony."

Jeff went over to the pony lot and put bridles on Ginger and Snowball.

"Okey hates to see Snowball and Ginger go," said Uncle Chick. "Them two never lifted a foot or caused any trouble in the five years since we've had 'em. Them ponies are so glad to see us each morning they walk over and get right in the harness."

"Do they know what you tell them?" asked Tina.

"They know more than a lot of people do," said Uncle Chick. "They go right up to that buggy to be hitched. And when they come out, they know just where to go and when to turn at the tipple, to get out of the way when Okey un-hooks 'em. Inside the mine, if there's bad slate overhead, they won't budge an inch. They seem to know a rockfall might kill 'em. Okey will sure miss 'em when they're gone. But they need a long rest now. That's why I'm sending them back to Gramp."

Jeff brought Ginger and Snowball out of the lot. "We got to hurry back, Uncle Chick, so we won't be late for school," said Jeff.

"Just a minute," said Uncle Chick. "If your dad wants to start a pony mine, Gramp will lease him that one over yonder. Some fellow started it a while back, and then up and left. The coal seam's thirty-six inches there and pretty good."

"Dad likes the big mine," said Jeff. "He don't want to go back to pick and shovel, he said. He'd rather work with machinery."

"I know how he feels," said Uncle Chick, "but he wants to feed his family, don't he? And since he's laid off now, I thought . . ."

"Dad says ponies are on their way out and big machinery is coming in," said Jeff.

"Yes, to displace the men," said Uncle Chick. "You tell him *the small mines will be here for a long time to come.* Every time the big mines lay men off, they're bound to go to work in the little mines—or starve. They can make work for themselves and be independent."

Jeff shook his head, feeling sad inside. He could see both sides and he did not know what the answer was.

The next minute the children heard Okey's "Hup!" again. There came Diamond out of the entry, then Bright Eyes, and a loaded coal car behind. The ponies had to pull hard up the sloping ramp to the dumping place on the tipple. Okey shouted, they stopped, Okey pulled the clevis pin which detached the harness from the coal car, and they stepped to one side out of the way. Okey pushed the buggy on ahead, where it tipped over and dumped the coal into the waiting truck below.

"Fine! Fine!" called Uncle Chick, climbing up the tipple ladder. "They're working like veterans!" He patted Diamond on the head.

Tina climbed up and put her arms around Bright Eyes' neck.

"Was Bright Eyes scared in the mine, Okey?" she asked.

"Scared?" Okey laughed. "That pony scared? Scared o' what?"

"Scared of bats . . . and rats . . ." said Tina. "Scared of the dark!"

Okey roared with laughter.

"Uncle Chick, can't a new pony get scared in the dark?" asked Tina.

"They don't like it too well at first—to go in the dark

mine," said Uncle Chick. "You have to lead them into start, and coax them a bit. After a trip or two, they seem to like it. In a week's time, Bright Eyes will think he's been a mine pony all his life."

"But oh—it's so black-dark in the mine!" Tina remembered how she had felt herself. She put her arms around the pony's neck again. She whispered in his ear, "If you don't like it, Bright Eyes, you just give Okey a swift kick!"

The children rode back on Snowball and Ginger and put them in Grandpa's barn. Then they ran off to school and got there just as the last bell rang.

"Oh, I hope nothing happens to Bright Eyes!" said Tina, as they were taking off their wraps.

"So do I," said Jeff.

It was only a week later that it happened. Jeff came tearing in the house with the news.

"I saw Okey in the pick-up!" panted Jeff. "He's going to Mapleton for the vet. Something's happened to Bright Eyes!"

"Oh *no!*" cried Tina. "You mean Diamond, not Bright Eyes. Diamond is the wild one."

"Okey said Bright Eyes, and he's hurt bad," said Jeff.

"I bet Okey was mean and Bright Eyes kicked him," said Tina. "I just know Bright Eyes don't like Okey one bit. And I don't either."

"Okey didn't get kicked," said Jeff. "It's Bright Eyes, I tell you. They think his leg is broke."

"What happened?" asked Daddy.

"Okey said Bright Eyes went crazy," said Jeff. "He kicked his harness off and banged into the shuttle buggy and broke one of his hind legs."

"Oh *no!* I don't believe it!" Tina began to cry.

"Okey wanted to shoot him," Jeff went on, "but Uncle Chick sent him for the vet."

Jeff and Tina and Daddy were at Grandpa's when Uncle

Chick drove up in his truck. There in the back lay Bright Eyes, with his leg in a splint. It took the three men and the vet to lift him out of the truck on a board and carry him into the stall.

"Did Okey whip him, Uncle Chick?" asked Tina, after the vet went away. "I bet Okey was mean and made Bright Eyes mad."

"It wasn't that way at all," said Uncle Chick. "Now if it had been Diamond, I wouldn't have been surprised. But you never can tell about these quiet ponies. Sometimes they surprise you. The ponies started running up the chute. Okey yelled but Bright Eyes didn't get out of the way in time. The coal car rolled and before it flipped over, it hit him on the leg and hurt it bad. He was in pain and kicked a lot . . . We had a hard time getting him quiet."

"This means the end for old Bright Eyes," said Daddy.

"The end of what?" asked Tina.

Daddy hated to tell her, but he had to.

"It's hard to save a pony with a broken leg," he said. "Usually it's better to put them out of the way. Even if his leg heals, Bright Eyes may never be able to work again."

"The vet don't think it's broken," said Uncle Chick. "He thinks it's just turned, and badly bruised and cut."

"The vet said to let him rest for a month, and then he'd be as good as new," added Jeff.

"That's fine," said Daddy. "Let's hope he gets well."

Before she went home, Tina went in the stall to see Bright
Eyes. The pony was lying down on a bed of hay, covered
with a blanket, his eyes closed. Tina was afraid to touch him.
She just leaned over and whispered.

"You didn't like it there in tne black-dark, did you?" she
said. "You kicked to let them know how you felt. Too bad
you hurt yourself so badly."

The pony did not open his eyes or look at her.

"I'll come by every day after school and take care of you,"
Tina went on. "And remember this—you won't have to go
back in the mine to work any more. My daddy said so. As
soon as your leg gets well, you'll be my pet. Do you hear me,
Bright Eyes?"

Tina and Jeff followed Daddy and hurried home. As they
passed the Murphys' house, they saw Mrs. Murphy on the
back porch.

"Supper's ready, Peggy and Mike," Mrs. Murphy called
out. "Come on in and get your ham and eggs!"

Peggy ran out to the gate first and called to Tina, *"We're*
having ham and eggs for supper! Are you?"

Tina shook her head. "No," she said.

She ran straight home and said to Mama, "The Murphys
are having ham and eggs for supper, Peggy said so!"

Mama laughed.

"Mrs. Murphy said so too!"

"Ham and eggs, my goodness!" said Mama. "And Pat

laid off six months already! Plenty imagination they're having, that's sure."

"What are we having, Mama?" asked Tina.

"Potato soup," said Mama. "Good and nourishing too."

.

On Sunday afternoon, Mama said Jeff and Tina could go to the hospital to see Uncle Jack. Uncle Chick came by in Uncle Jack's car to pick them up. Grandma went along.

Tina had not been to Mapleton for a long time. It was fun to ride up the steep hill out of the coal camp valley to the big town on the highway that led to Charleston. It was exciting to see the big stores and churches, the post office and fire department, though they were all closed on Sunday. Soon they came to the red brick hospital. Uncle Chick parked the car and they went in.

Grandma had her arms so full of packages, Tina had to help her carry them.

They went up the elevator and down a long hall. They came into a big ward, with many beds along the sides. The men in them were sleeping, talking or laughing. Which one was Uncle Jack?

Grandma headed for a bed in the far corner. Tina tried to pull her back. That was not the right place, for there was a pretty young lady there, leaning over the man in the bed. Grandma must have made a mistake. Tina pulled her by the arm and said, "That's not Uncle Jack! Let's go find him."

"Oh yes it is," said Grandma, dropping her packages at the foot of the bed.

The pretty young lady turned around. To her surprise, Tina saw that it was Miss Sanford, her teacher at school.

"Why . . . why . . . do you know my Uncle Jack?" asked Tina.

"Do I *know* him?" asked Miss Sanford. "I sure do."

Uncle Jack laughed and caught Miss Sanford's hand. "Helen and I are the best of friends," he said.

"Helen? Who's that?" asked Tina.

"Helen Sanford," said Uncle Jack. "Miss Sanford's name is *Helen.*"

Tina looked at her teacher and saw that her cheeks were very pink. Grandma and Jeff brought chairs and they all sat down. Grandma opened her bundles. She had cookies and fruit for Uncle Jack, pajamas and bedroom slippers.

"Oh, Uncle Jack," said Tina. "I couldn't bring you any flowers. Grandma's dahlias were frozen up."

"O.K., honey," said Uncle Jack.

It didn't seem like Uncle Jack at all, this strange man with his shoulder and arm in a cast, lying propped up in bed. He kept talking to "Helen" most of the time, while Grandma and the children listened.

Jeff told him about Bright Eyes' accident, and he grew sober.

"Ponies!" said Uncle Jack. "Who wants to use ponies in a

mine? Have you heard about auger-mining? That's the latest thing! Two men and a big machine can get out more coal than twenty men with the old machines, and they never have to go inside the mine at all. They strip off all the top soil and rock, and let the machine bore holes into the side of the mountain and twist the coal out."

"But Jack," said Miss Sanford, "I thought you were through with mining. Hasn't this accident taught you a lesson?"

Jack laughed and turned to his mother.

"Shall I give up mining and find some other kind of a job, Mom?"

Grandma looked sad and said, "That is for you to decide— you and Helen."

Grandma called her "Helen" too. On the way home, Grandma asked Tina, "How do you think you'll like your Aunt Helen?"

Tina did not know what to say. She liked Miss Sanford for a teacher, but could she ever learn to call her "Helen"— "Aunt Helen"?

Chapter Six

WINTER

MAMA lighted a kerosene lamp and set it on the table beside the window. "So Walter can see when he comes in," she said.

She looked down the road at the row of houses below her own. The white snow made them look dingier than ever. A heavy snow had fallen and the electric power had gone off.

"Soon all the houses will be boarded up," Mama said. "The Davises went first. Soon the others will go too."

She put a shawl around her shoulders, sat down and took baby Letty on her lap. The baby had been crying all day. Winter was always the hardest time of the year.

86

A truck pulled up outside and stopped with a jerk. A man got out and pulled a heavy sack of coal down. He carried it to the coal shed and dumped it. Then he went back for a second sack. The truck went on. Mama heard the back door open.

"That you, Walter?" she called. "Did you bring the coal?"

"Yes, Mary Kate," said Daddy. "I brought in a scoop bucket full."

"Fill up the stove then," said Mama. "Fire's most out. House is freezin'—and Christina sick."

Daddy began to fix the fire. He shook down the ashes. Coal gas and smoke filled the room as he poured coal dust from the scoop bucket on the live coals.

"What—no lumps?" asked Mama. "Only slack?"

"Best I could get under the snow," said Daddy.

He forgot to close the draft at the bottom when he put the coal in. Flames shot up toward the ceiling, right in his face. He closed the lid promptly and set the drafts.

"You say Tina's sick?" he asked. "What's wrong with her?"

"Teacher carried her home in her car, long about noon," said Mama. "Teacher said she was too weak to walk home."

"Teacher? Teacher?" asked Daddy. "Who do you mean?"

"Miss Sanford," said Mama. "Helen—don't you know? Ben Sanford's girl. Ben, your buddy in the mine, before he got hurt so bad. He's in a wheel-chair now all the time."

"Ben's girl is grown up and teaching school?" asked Daddy.

"Yes," said Mama. "She's got big ideas too—you'd never guess she was brought up in a coal camp herself. She said the kids had no business comin' to school with their stomachs empty—and no breakfast. Christina must of fainted at school, or fell over, or somethin' . . . Helen Sanford blamed me."

"What'd you tell her?" asked Daddy.

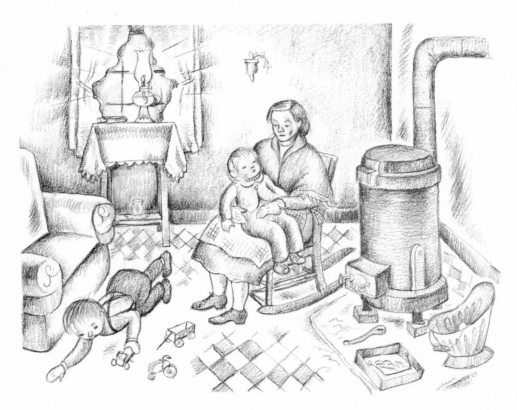

"Told her I didn't have a thing in the world to feed 'em," said Mama. "Told her we was lucky to manage one meal a day right now."

"What'd she say to that?"

"She got real mad," said Mama. "And do you know what she said about Jack? Said Jack was givin' up mining for good and all. Said her pa got crippled for life and she wasn't going to let the same thing happen to Jack. Said Jack had had his warning . . . Now what do you make of that?"

"Sounds like there's something between them two," said Daddy. "Then what did she do?"

"She up and left," said Mama.

"No breakfast! My kids—no breakfast!" Daddy sat down quickly in a chair. "I know how it feels—as if the bottom of your stomach has dropped out. Those sacks of coal were the heaviest I ever lifted." He paused. "And I never used to get tired at all when I worked sixteen hours a day."

Mama put the baby in her crib and came out again.

"Celia, where did you put that head o' cabbage?" she called. "I'll cook it now we got some coal dust to cook with."

Celia came in from the bedroom.

"Bring any groceries, Dad?" she asked. "Bring any milk?"

Her father turned on her angrily. "You think I've been to the grocery store and bought it out?" he asked. "You know, Celia, my credit's all used up at the company store. They won't give us a penny of scrip. My rockin' chair money ran out last month. Where you been? Ain't you heard the coal mine's closed down?" Walter Wilson, like all the miners, referred to unemployment compensation as "rocking chair money."

"I thought maybe they'd trust you for a can or two of condensed milk," said Celia. "My baby's hungry for milk."

"Jeff and Tina and Ronnie have forgot what milk tastes like," said Mama. "No meat or milk since October. Only bread, potatoes and beans for the last two weeks. Today for a change, we'll have cabbage."

"Feed the baby cabbage, Celia!" Daddy laughed, but it wasn't funny at all. Celia hung her head and went out of the kitchen. She did not like Daddy's jokes.

"No good going to the mine superintendent," said Daddy. "He said it was all our own fault gettin' in a fix like this. Said no matter how high wages the miners get, they never save anything, and when hard times come, not one of 'em can live a week . . . Guess that's about it."

The kitchen warmed up as the fire caught the coal dust. Daddy tipped his chair back against the wall. He turned on the battery radio beside him and soft music began to play. Daddy began to feel better.

"Where's my girl?" he called out. "Where's that little ole Teeny girl? Come here, Teeny, let me see how sick you are."

A stir was heard in the bedroom, then the swift patter of bare feet on the cold linoleum floor. The tousle-headed figure of a girl came running into the room.

"Daddy! Daddy!" She ran to her father and leaned on his shoulder. "Daddy, Daddy, did you get you a job? Is the mine gonna open tomorrow?"

"They'll open up when the company gets more orders for coal," said Daddy. "They'll take all their men back again."

"I'm glad," said Tina. "Tomorrow?"

"Not just yet, sugar pie," said Daddy, "but one of these days soon. Hey, you kid, what kind of big winter coat is this you're wearin'?"

Tina began to laugh.

"Big winter coat?" she said. "You know I don't have a big winter coat. It's the comfort offa my bed. I had to wrap it round and round me, to git me warm. I was so cold, I felt like an icicle. Gee! It's nice and warm in here. Let me sit on your lap."

Big girl that she was, going on ten, Tina jumped on her father's lap and curled up. He folded his arms around her as if he would keep her from harm. He decided to tell her the truth. She was old enough to know.

"When a mine closes down, Tina, it's bound to mean hardship," said Daddy. "Not only for us, but for every family in the coal camp."

"What's hardship, Daddy?" asked Tina.

"No coal, no pay. No pay, no food," said Daddy. "That's hardship. All miners know hardship at one time or another when the men are laid off."

"Does it mean no treats in your bucket, Daddy?" asked Tina.

"Yes, no candy, cake or gum," said Daddy.

"No trips to the dime store in Mapleton?" asked Tina. "No show on Saturdays?"

"That's about it, sugar," said Daddy.

"But the mine will open up, won't it?" asked Tina.

Daddy began to rumple her hair.

"Big ole baby you," he said softly. "Better not let your little brother see you settin' on my lap. He'll fight you and bust your head open."

"I don't feel like fightin' today, Daddy," said the girl.

"Next time that Peggy Murphy hits you, you yell for me and I'll come flyin'," said Daddy. "You don't feel good, sugar?"

"I'm tired—not sick—just tired," said Tina. "So tired I couldn't stand up no more in school . . . at the blackboard. Didn't git my arithmetic done, the numbers kept jumpin' so . . ."

"I know how it feels, honey," said Daddy.

"But Daddy, you didn't answer me," said Tina. "Is the mine gonna open up *soon?*" The girl looked up at him and her face showed its pallor and thinness in the lamplight.

"Sure, sugar," the man said. "Purty soon."

"Is the whistle gonna blow while I'm still in bed in the

mornin'?" asked the girl. "And will you go off down the hill before it's light? And will you save me a treat in your lunch bucket?"

"Not tomorrow," said Daddy. "I gotta go scrape up some more coal for us tomorrow, if the snow is gone. And more cabbage maybe."

"Helen Sanford wanted to know why the kids missed so much school," said Mama, coming in. "I told her the truth —Jeff's shoes are plumb wore out, and Christina's soles is flappin'."

"You're gonna go to work again and buy us all some new shoes, ain't you, Daddy?" said Tina. Her voice was warm with hope and trust.

"Sure, honey," said Daddy. "Purty soon now."

"Mrs. Krupa came to see me, Walter," said Mama. "She said I ought to go on Welfare, like all the other miners' families. I told her I just couldn't."

"We're not that low yet," said Daddy.

That night Celia and the children went to bed early, but Mama and Daddy sat up to talk.

"Things can't go on like this, Walter," said Mama.

"I know it," said Daddy.

"If we don't go on Welfare, maybe we ought to clear out like the Davises and go away somewhere," said Mama.

"I wouldn't know where to go," said Daddy. "I haven't enough education to get a job in town. I've lived here all my life—it's the only life I know."

"Can't you get a job in some other mine, one of the other big ones?" asked Mama.

"They wouldn't take me," said Daddy. "I'm past forty and I've got silicosis. Every man that's worked twenty years in a mine has got it. I'd be afraid to let them take X-rays—I know what they'd find. Besides, I have no car to drive a long way to another mine."

"But you can't wait forever for the company to call you back," said Mama.

"When they get more coal orders, they will," said Daddy. "I want to stick by them and get my pension when I'm sixty. I'm fifty now—it won't be long."

"But in the meantime, we've got to eat," said Mama.

"Yes," said Daddy. "It means mollygrub then. I saw a sign in the window of the company store today. There's to be a distribution of surplus government food tomorrow. At the Baptist church, at 4 p.m."

Mama looked shocked. "And you want me to go?"

"Why not?" said Daddy. "That surplus food is all that is keeping the miners from starving. My buddy told me you can get free flour and rice and other food. We haven't much choice in the matter. Christina fainted in school today. She hasn't been getting enough to eat. It's not begging."

Mama shook her head. "I'd be ashamed to go."

"You are too proud, I guess," said Daddy.

"No more proud than you," said Mama. "You won't go to work in my brother Chick's pony mine! Why not? You're too proud—that's the only reason. The big mine makes you feel like a big shot, so you 'stick by the company,' no matter if your family starves."

Daddy did not speak right away.

"You're right, Mary Kate," he said. "It's pride—we're

both too proud and our children suffer for it. Will you go and get some of that mollygrub, if I start work in Chick's pony mine?"

Mama said yes, and Daddy took her in his arms.

Tina stayed out of school for several days and spent most of her time in bed. One day she got up, put her old jacket on and went outside. But the cold wind chilled her, so she soon returned. The fire in the heater had gone out, but coals in the open grate in the bedroom were alive and red. Tina went to the grate and bent over, rubbing her hands to warm them.

Celia was in the kitchen, scrubbing the floor, and had the outside door open. As she opened the bedroom door to mop the door sill, the wind blew in, caught Tina's thin cotton skirt and fanned it across the hot coals. The next minute, the flames shot up toward the little girl's face.

"Oh! Oh! My skirt's on fire!" Her voice was a shriek of pain.

Daddy, in the front room, threw his paper down and ran. The next minute, before she could think, he had the girl down on the floor and was rolling a rug around her. When she looked up, they were all staring at her—Daddy, Mama, Celia and the baby, Jeff and little Ronnie. They were all scared and crying. After Daddy lifted her to the bed, he found that the palms of his hands were badly burned.

Tina cried and cried because the burn hurt so bad. Mama's screams brought Mrs. Bryant running, and they took her clothes off. Her right leg was burned from knee to thigh. Mrs. Bryant found some salve and they put it on. That night Mrs. Bryant sent over a folding cot, so Tina could sleep alone instead of with Celia and the baby.

The news of the mishap spread quickly. The neighbors came in to see if they could help. Mrs. Murphy came, wrung her hands and cried. Mrs. Diehl mixed an old-world recipe and they put it on the burn. Mrs. Tucker and Virgil stopped on their way to Mapleton. Mrs. Tucker offered to take Tina to a doctor, but Mama said she had no money for doctor bills.

"It will heal in time," said Mama, little dreaming how long it would take.

People kept coming in. Tina didn't know she had so many friends. They all felt sorry for her.

Hilda Krupa came with her mother and brought a bag of candy. Dave Hurley hobbled in on his crutches and offered to lend them to Tina when she was able to walk. Miss Sanford—"Helen"—brought letters from Tina's class at school, and left her school books so she could keep up with her lessons. Even Peggy Murphy came and said she was sorry she had picked on Tina and given her a black eye.

All the kinfolk came. Uncle Chick and Aunt Effie brought the cousins, Trig, Dede and little Cindy. They brought her cards, candy and gum. Grandpa and Grandma came every day, and Grandma always brought cookies. They all came but Uncle Jack, who was still in the hospital.

The days were long for Tina, lying in bed. Sometimes Mama propped her up on pillows, so she could look out the window. The slate dump was covered with snow now, and after school she watched the children sliding down on sleds or boards or cardboards. Sometimes Jeff slid on Mama's coal shovel. By balancing the handle in front, he could go down fast. One day when Mama asked for it, the coal shovel was gone. Jeff had left it at the bottom of the hill and had to go and look for it.

One day Tina asked about the ponies. "I've got to get up," she said. "Poor Bright Eyes with his broken leg! I promised him I'd come and see him every day."

"Gramp and I are taking good care of Bright Eyes," said Jeff. "The vet says we can soon take the splint off."

Now there was more to eat and Tina was not as hungry as before. Mama went to the Baptist church each time the surplus food was given out. She got beans, cornmeal, flour, butter and sometimes other foods. Once the churches in Charleston sent down a windfall of canned milk, canned peas and some sugar. Other women, besides Mama, who had been too proud to go before, forgot their pride so that their families might eat.

Daddy started to work in the pony mine with Uncle Chick's men. He felt happier now, for he was earning again. Each night he brought Tina a treat in his bucket. Each night he sat by Tina's bed and talked. But it didn't last long. For suddenly Daddy started staying at home again all day long.

What was it now? Had Uncle Chick's mine closed down? Tina hated to ask. It was Jeff who told her. The punch mine was flooded with water and no one could work. Jeff had brought all the ponies up to Grandpa's barn. Uncle Chick and his men were trying to pump the mine out. They pumped each day and got the water out, but it came right back in again. Nobody could work knee-deep in water.

But a happy day came when Uncle Jack was allowed to leave the hospital. Daddy said, "Let's celebrate! Even if we can't work, we can have a little fun. We all need it." He told Jeff to ask all the neighbors to come in at eight o'clock that evening for a party.

"Shall I ask the Murphys to come?" asked Jeff.

"Why, sure," said Mama. "They cause us lots of trouble, but they're our neighbors and we want them too."

When Uncle Jack came, Tina hardly knew him because he looked different. The cast was gone but he still had his arm in a sling. Mama had a hard time explaining about Tina's burn.

"I know, I know!" said Uncle Jack. "Helen told me, but I never guessed it was so bad. You never took her to a doctor . . . and she's been in bed all this time!"

Mama was crying so, she could not answer.

Uncle Jack leaned over and kissed Tina's cheek.

"O.K., cherry pie," he said. "I'm going back to work again, and we'll get you well as soon as we can."

At the party Tina sat up in a chair and never got tired at all. She wore a new dress that Uncle Jack and Miss Sanford got for her, and she looked pretty even though she was very thin. Tina watched the people as they came in, bringing coffee, cold drinks and cakes and cookies. There were the Bryants, the Hurleys and the Watsons; the Krupas, the Collinses and all the kinfolk. Then came the Tuckers with Virgil and Rita, followed by the Murphys with Peggy and Mike. They were all dressed in their best clothes. Pat Murphy brought his violin, sat down to tune up, then began to play. The women set the furniture back to make room for square dancing.

The little coal camp house was alive with bright lights in every room. And its walls were fairly bursting with happiness and merriment, as the dancers whirled around. Some of the men sat on the back porch and "mined coal" in conversation. The children frolicked, ate and drank, and had the time of their lives.

Everybody forgot that the mine was closed down, and that there were few pennies to rattle in their pocket-books. Everyone forgot how close a miner's family can come to starvation, to mishap and danger. The breath of life was strong in them all, as they put their worries aside and deliberately chose to be happy.

Tina watched the dancing and wished that she could dance too. When Uncle Jack came and asked her to try it, she took a few steps with him. But the old burn pained her so badly, she had to sit down again. Miss Sanford came up and waved a kiss to Tina as she and Uncle Jack danced away.

"Helen!" said Tina to herself. "Aunt Helen."

She had loved her as a teacher. Could she love her still more, if she became a member of the family?

Chapter Seven

DISASTER

"Where's my girl? Where's my Teeny girl?"

Daddy came striding up the hill from the mine ahead of the other men. He swung his lunch bucket invitingly.

Ronnie ran to get it, but Daddy said "No. The treat is for girls only. The treat is for Tina."

It was the first time she had left the house. Tina ran to meet Daddy coming home from the big mine. She opened his bucket and found a big fat chocolate bar for a treat.

"Oh Daddy! How wonderful!" cried Tina. "I'll give half to Ronnie." She broke it in half and she and Ronnie gobbled it up.

When they got home, there was Jeff carrying the two buckets of Daddy's bath water up the back steps.

With the coming of spring, things began to look better again. Daddy and many of the other men had been called back to work in the big mine. Now the mine whistle blew for the changes of shifts each day. Now the air was filled with coal dust again, and the busy coal-cars went chugging in and out of the valley behind the smoky steam engine every day. Life resumed its usual pattern, the strain left the wom-

en's faces, and the happiness was reflected even in the children.

When Tina was able to walk again, Grandma Ferris asked her to come and stay for a week before she went back to school. Tina clapped her hands when Mama said she could go. It was always fun at Grandma's house, and she would be near the ponies.

Would Bright Eyes remember her? Now that the pony's leg was well again, would Bright Eyes give her a ride on his back?

There were so many things to do at Grandma's. When Tina stepped out of Uncle Jack's car, she smelled cookies baking. The kitchen was warm and sweet and spicy when she went in. She was just in time to help Grandma roll out the last batch. She cut the cookies in rounds with the cookie-cutter. She took them out of the oven when they were brown.

"Grandma, why do you always have cookies, and Mama none?" asked Tina. All her life Tina had come to Grandma's house and found cookies waiting.

"Gramp has his pension," said Grandma. "That gives us more money for groceries than your mama has when Daddy is out of work."

"Oh!" said Tina. *"No cookies* is one of the hardships, isn't it?"

"It doesn't hurt us to learn to do without things we want," said Grandma.

"Food, too?" asked Tina.

"Just the extras like cookies," said Grandma. "Other food is a necessity."

Tina heard a loud pounding on the roof.

"What's that, Grandma? A woodpecker?"

Grandma laughed. "Uncle Jack's a pretty big woodpecker, don't you think?"

"Is it Uncle Jack?" asked Tina. "What's he doing?"

"He and Gramp are putting new shingles on," said Grandma. "Jack is doing most of it. I won't let Gramp climb on the ladder."

"Can Uncle Jack pound with his broken arm?"

"Yes, it needs exercise to strengthen it," said Grandma.

"Can *I* help?" asked Tina.

"*You?* I should say not," said Grandma. "I don't want anything to happen to you while you're here. I'm going to feed you up and put a little flesh on your bones. You've grown so skinny, I'm afraid the wind will blow you away. You'll have to be stronger before you can go back to school."

The rat-a-tat-tat on the roof continued.

"Run out to the chicken coop and bring in the eggs," said Grandma.

Tina found six eggs in the nests and brought them in in her skirt. Grandma beat one of them into a glass of fresh milk. She gave it to Tina to drink.

"Oh! how good!" said Tina. "I could drink a gallon!"

"You will have it every day while you are here," said Grandma.

The very next morning Tina went out to see the ponies. To her joy and delight, Bright Eyes came running to meet her. Tina held out a lump of sugar. Bright Eyes nuzzled it first, then ate it. Tina put her arm around the pony's neck.

"You remember me, don't you, Bright Eyes?"

Grandpa helped the girl get on the pony's back and led him as she rode round the pasture.

"Will you take Bright Eyes back to the mine again?" asked Tina.

"His leg is still too stiff," said Grandpa. "The vet said it was a wonder he recovered. We had to get a new pony to work with Diamond—his name is Knot-Head! He's a hard-headed one!"

Tina did not dare to say how glad she was. She patted Bright Eyes on the back and loved him more than ever. Every morning and evening she rode the pony round the pasture. Soon the pony began to trot with her, and then to gallop. The pony was good and obedient and made no trouble at all.

In the evenings Tina did her lessons with Uncle Jack, who said, "Helen doesn't want you to miss a whole winter of school, so you must work hard to catch up."

Uncle Jack made the work seem like play, so it was fun. One by one the days went by. The trees were budding out and early blossoms were opening. The dark dinginess of winter began to fade away in the coal camp valley, with the brightness of the spring sunshine.

Then one day it was cloudy. Thick heavy clouds hung low in the valley. Dim lights shone in all the little houses, for it grew dark soon after midday. Then the rain began to fall, cold heavy drenching rain. Sometimes it would stop only to start in again with greater force. The feeling of spring vanished with the chill of cold.

Tina could not go home at the end of her week. Grandma did not want her to get wet and catch cold. It was better to stay inside, secure and dry in the warmth and comfort of the big heater stove. Uncle Jack had finished patching the roof just in time. There were no more leaks and Grandma was glad.

"You can't go home until the rains stop," said Grandma.

So day after day, Tina waited. Like Mama, Grandma had no telephone, so Tina could not talk to her family, and she began to feel homesick. Was Daddy still working at the big mine? Had Ronnie's front tooth come out, the one that was loose? Was baby Letty walking yet?

Uncle Chick came in now and then. He said all was well at home but gave no details. His entire concern was with the mines. He reported that all the pony mines were flooded with water, and none of them working. He had heard a rumor that Linden Number 3 was flooding too, but Grandpa and

Uncle Jack refused to believe it.

The rains kept on and on. They were so bad that most of the children stopped going to school. Uncle Jack brought this news from Helen Sanford. So Tina felt better about having to miss.

Then one morning, when Tina got up, she looked out of the window. Across the road, beyond Grandma's chicken house and yard, stood the big mountain of the slate dump, where she had had so many happy hours of play. Way, way up at the top, she had seen birch trees growing and wondered if she could climb up there and slide down. She had never tried it for fear of landing in Grandma's chicken yard or on the front porch in Grandpa's lap!

Now she could hardly believe her eyes. What had happened in the night?

The road was gone, the chicken house and yard were gone, Grandma's flower bed and the front porch were gone—covered up with slate. The whole big mountain of the slate dump had come sliding down! There were the birch trees now—just a little way up. They were bending over, all topsy-turvy.

Tina remembered the last time she had played at the top—how she and Jeff had thrown stones and tried to hit Grandpa's chimney. The rain, the rain—it had washed all the slate down. Her old fear returned. Was it going to cover up Grandpa's house and bury it?

Tina ran to the side window. There was the Krupas' house
a little higher up. The slate dump was coming down on it
too. It was over the roof in the back, and most of the yard
was gone. Were the Krupas up? Did they know the danger?
Where was Hilda? Tina wanted to tell her to hurry up and
get out . . .

She pulled on her clothes as quickly as she could and ran
downstairs. The rooms were dark there, those on the mountainside by the dump. Through the back kitchen windows

overlooking the valley, she had a fleeting glimpse of a red sun trying to rise. Was the rain over at last? Out through the side door Tina ran without looking back.

"Hey! Where are you going, sugar pie?"

A strong hand pulled her by the arm and dragged her back indoors.

"You can't go running off like that so early in the morning," said Uncle Jack's kindly voice.

"But Hilda—Hilda Krupa . . . I've got to wake her up, before the slate dump falls on her . . ."

"Now, now . . ." Uncle Jack brought Tina in the kitchen and put her in a chair.

Grandma was fixing breakfast just as usual. It was going to be diced potatoes fried with onions, ham and red gravy, hot biscuits and butter. Grandpa was shaving by the kitchen sink. Everything was just as usual. The sun came up over the mountain to the east and flooded the sky, as if trying to tell the people in the coal camp that the worst was over.

Was nobody going to do anything? Were Grandma and Grandpa going to sit still and let their house be covered up?

"But look!" cried Tina. "Look at the slate dump! It's coming right down on us. I want to go home, oh, I want to go home . . ." She began to cry as if her heart would break.

Grandma took her in her arms and quieted her. Then Grandma and Grandpa and Uncle Jack explained. As soon as it dried off a little, they were all going down to Christina's house in the valley. It looked as if the rain was over, and when the roads were dry enough, the mine company would send its trucks to haul the slate away.

The Krupas had already gone to their kinfolk, and other families in the endangered houses were going soon. The slate would not slide any more if the rain stopped.

"It won't cover Gramp's house up?" asked Tina.

"No," said Grandpa. "It was a close shave and we're lucky. Mine is the nicest house with the best view of the valley. I don't want to move any more than you do."

So they all went down the hill to Christina's house in the valley to stay until the slate was removed. Uncle Jack went off to stay at Uncle Chick's in Crabapple Hollow, and Mama made up the davenport in the front room for Grandma and Grandpa.

Tina was happy to be at home again. A few days passed happily and calmly, and then the quiet was shattered by the unexpected.

"What time is it, Mama?" asked Tina one day.

"Almost three-thirty," said Mama. "The whistle will blow soon."

"Can I go to meet Daddy?" asked the girl.

"Not in this rain," said Mama. It was raining again. The spring rains had never been so heavy.

"You stay inside and keep dry," said Grandma. "We don't want you to catch cold."

Dinner was nearly ready and Mama was heating water for Daddy's bath. The family waited and talked.

Mama looked at the clock. "Why, it's almost four," she said. "I didn't hear the whistle blow. And Daddy's not here." She turned to Grandma.

Suddenly a loud blast sounded. It was the mine whistle, and it kept on and on. Mama and Grandma looked at each other, and Tina saw fear in their faces.

"Something's happened at the mine," whispered Mama. "The day shift hasn't come off."

"The disaster whistle blows only for one of three things—a slate fall, a flood or an explosion," said Grandma.

Suddenly a siren was heard. Jeff and Tina ran to the front window. Down the hill road from Mapleton came an ambulance at top speed. It turned at the corner and went down to the big tipple. Several other speeding cars followed.

"Where's Daddy?" asked Tina. "Why doesn't he come home?"

Grandpa came out to the kitchen. "I'll go down to the mine," he said.

"Can I go too, Gramp?" asked Tina.

Mama reached for her coat and scarf, but Grandpa took them from her and hung them back in the closet.

"None of you can go," he said. "No one but Jeff. If there's trouble, they don't want women and children around. We'll let you know when we find out anything."

As soon as Grandpa left, Mama hurried over to Mrs. Bryant's house to see if she had heard any news by telephone.
After a while she came back.

"The mine is flooded and the men are trapped," she said.
"They were cut off at one o'clock, when water broke through
the roof, bringing mud and rocks with it." She turned to
Grandma. "There's that refuse pond high on the mountainside. They dammed it up for a dumping ground for waste
from the coal washing machine. All this rain filled it to over-
flowing. The weight of the water collapsed the four hundred
foot of rock and earth that formed a wall between the pond
and the mine passageway. The mine's full of water."

Mama began to cry and Grandma put her arms around
her.

"They'll get the men out," said Grandma. "Oh, how many
times I've been through this kind of thing before! Each time,
I think I can never take it again, but each time, God gives me
the strength I need. Don't lose heart, Mary Kate. Walter
will come out safe. Keep your faith—that will help."

Tina knew Grandma was right, so she stopped crying too.
They all sat at the window and watched cars go down the
hill toward the mine. It was still raining hard.

About five o'clock Jeff came home with news.

"They're going to get them out!" he cried excitedly.
"There's lots of people there. They've got pumps running
to pump the water out. Seven mine inspectors came and went

in with the two foremen to hunt for another way for the men to come out. The main hallway is completely blocked. Karl Krupa, Hilda's father, who was laid off six months ago, says he knows how to get them out. He was section foreman in there for fifteen years. He's taking a bunch of men in to try to find it."

"Have they heard from the men?" asked Mama. "Are they still alive?"

"They haven't heard anything yet," said Jeff. "But a man

told me they are going to bore a hole down to them from the top of the mountain, for food and a telephone wire. They think they know about where the men are. They're waiting now for a bulldozer to come to cut a road through the trees and bushes to the top."

"Oh, that'll be too slow," said Mama. "It'll be too late."

About seven o'clock Grandpa came back. Mama met him at the door.

"Have they heard from the men?" she asked. "Are they still alive?"

"The Mine Superintendent says he's sure they are," said Grandpa. "He said he won't call it a disaster because he feels sure the men are alive and unhurt. He said the dispatcher was in contact with the motor crew and the mine foreman just before the power went off, and all the men in the mine were reported to be at the face. That's farther in and higher up than the point of the break—where the water came in. They've pumped the water out, but it's left behind a river of jelly-like sludge that's hard to get through."

"How long will it take?" asked Mama.

"The Mine Superintendent said that rescue is still twenty-four hours away, at least," said Grandpa.

"He'll be there all night," said Mama, her eyes filling with tears.

"Waiting and doing nothing is hardest of all," said Grandma.

"There's nothing any of us can do," said Grandpa. "Everything is being done that can be done. Chick and Jack are down there helping. I must go back." He took the sandwiches and coffee Mama made and left.

That night no one wanted to go to bed. The children fell asleep in their chairs, so Mama tucked them in bed. Lights were on in all the company houses, and cars kept coming and going. Toward morning Mama and Grandma lay down to get some rest.

In the morning Grandpa came back. The news was just the same, everything possible was being done. No message had come from the men, but it was believed they were safe. The rain slackened and that made the rescue work easier.

Tina felt it was the longest day she had ever lived through. Jeff and Grandpa stayed at the mine, coming home only for food. Mama and Celia decided to do a big washing, so Grandma helped. Neighbors stopped in, equally tense and worried, asking questions and making predictions. Ronnie kept asking, "When is Daddy coming home?"

Tina sat in a chair by the side window and watched. She wanted to be the first one to see Daddy when he came. She wanted to run to meet him. "There won't be any treat this time," she said. "I'll let Daddy eat my treat while he's waiting to be dug out."

Grandma smiled.

Another night passed and another day came. Before break-fast, while it was still dark, Mrs. Bryant came in and said she was going to the mine. Mama put on her coat and scarf, and told the children to get their wraps. "I've waited long enough," she said. "I'm going down there too. Jeff and Tina, you come along. If anything's happened to Daddy, we want to be there."

Everything was different and strange at Linden Number 3. Cars were parked all around the mine buildings and a

row of ambulances stood waiting. People stood around talking and waiting outside and inside the mine buildings. Nobody seemed to know anything. Jeff went off with Cliff
Crouse and Sammy Blagg, but Tina stayed with her mother.

"I couldn't stand it to stay at home any longer," said Mrs.
Bryant.

"Something's bound to happen today," said Mama, "and
I want to be here to know the worst—or the best." She wiped
her eyes and tried to smile.

Inside the waiting room next to the lamp house, there was
a fire in a coal stove. A row of Mapleton Boy Scouts with
stretchers sat on a bench waiting in case they were needed in
rescue.

"Twenty-four lamps have been checked out," the lamp
man kept telling people who came up. "So we know there
are twenty-four men missing."

Tina felt tired, so she leaned against Mama's shoulder. She
must have fallen asleep, for suddenly she was wakened.
Mama had jumped up and she and Mrs. Bryant were rushing
toward the mine office. A messenger from the mine had just
gone in. Newspaper reporters crowded close, and after a
short time, the general manager of the mine came out.

"Gentlemen," he said, "the workers have been located and
all twenty-four are in good physical condition!"

The reporters crowded closer to get details.

"Karl Krupa, a former foreman, took a small crew of nine

into an abandoned section of the mine in search of a by-pass. They found it and reached the men, who are now on their way out."

A cheer went up from reporters and bystanders, as everybody hurried to the mine portal. Tina held tightly to Mama's hand, as they all crowded close. They waited a long time. Then they saw the men coming.

Dirty and hungry, but uninjured, the happy group of trapped miners walked into the cold light of dawn and sniffed the fresh air.

"Gimme a cigarette!" begged Ben Hurley, the first man out. "Two days since I had a smoke!"

"Coffee, a cup of coffee!" shouted Henry Bryant, as he fell into his wife's waiting arms.

Then Tina saw Daddy. She knew him even if his face was black. He looked up into the sky and said for all to hear, "I never thought I'd see the light of day again. Thank the good Lord."

The next minute Tina was in his arms and Mama too. Mama took his black face between her two hands and kissed him in front of everybody.

All around there was a great hubbub. Waiting women took black-faced men in their arms and cried tears of relief and happiness. Newsmen came close and took pictures. Karl Krupa was a hero for bringing the men out. The mine chief from Charleston, who had spent two days and nights in rescue work without rest, was another. And Willie Johnson, a colored miner, who had told jokes and sung songs to the imprisoned men, was a third. They were all given a warm and loving welcome.

The rain was over and a warm sun came out, as Daddy and Mama and Tina and Jeff walked back up the hill, followed by Grandpa.

Daddy gave his bucket to Tina.

"Don't you want your treat, Teeny girl?" he asked.

"But I thought you ate it all up," said Tina, "when you had to go hungry so long."

"No," said Daddy, "I saved it for you."

Tina opened the bucket and ate the stale, mine-soaked sandwich she found there.

"It's the best treat I ever tasted!" she said.

Chapter Eight

SUMMER

"Oh, Gramp! I can't believe it!" said Tina, hugging him tightly. "I can have Bright Eyes for my very own?"

Grandpa Ferris nodded.

"That stiff leg will keep him from ever being a good mine pony," said Grandpa. "He can never work again."

Tina put her arm around the pony's neck.

"Do you hear that, Bright Eyes?" she whispered. "You are my pony now. You don't have to go in the mine any more."

Tina was feeling stronger now than she had been all winter. Jeff and Uncle Jack built a shed for Bright Eyes in the backyard. By day the pony grazed in the yard, eating the grass and weeds. All the children in the street came to have rides. Bright Eyes was gentle and let them do as they pleased with him.

After the rains were over, spring came quickly to the coal camp. The mine company trucks hauled all the slate away from the houses on the mountain road. The grass turned green and the trees put out fresh new leaves. People began planting flower beds and gardens. Daddy took down the coal

heater and moved it out to the back porch.

One day when the children came home from school, Mama met them at the door with buckets in her hand. "Go get water," she said.

Tina hated wash-day, but she and Jeff went to the spigot in Mrs. Murphy's yard, crossing three other yards to get there. Queenie went along, sniffing at their heels. Mrs. Murphy was getting ready to wash tomorrow too, so Peggy was at the spigot, filling her buckets. Peggy did not hurry, so Jeff and Tina stood patiently and waited.

Queenie began to growl. She saw the Murphys' cat and went after it. The cat arched its back and spat, then turned and ran. Cat and dog disappeared under the Murphys' house.

"You take that dog of yours out of our yard!" screamed Peggy.

Jeff called Queenie, but she did not come. Peggy left her buckets, took a stick and threw it under the house, trying to hit the dog.

"Come now, quick!" said Jeff. "Let's get our water and go. Queenie can take care of herself."

When Peggy came back to the spigot, Jeff and Tina were gone. They had learned how to avoid a quarrel with Peggy.

Before they went to school next day, the wash water was on the stove in a Number 4 tub heating. Washing was an all-day job for both Mama and Celia. When Tina came home that afternoon, Mama's clotheslines were full of clothes, and so was a long one of Mrs. Bryant's next door. Mama was scrubbing the back porch and steps with lye water to make them white and clean.

"Run and see if the clothes are dry, Tina," called Mama.

But Tina had other things on her mind. Hilda Krupa and cousin Dede had come home with her to help fix up Tina's summer playhouse. The little coal shed out by the front fence had been emptied of coal, so the girls decided to clean it up.

They brought buckets of water and scrubbed and scrubbed. It took a long time to get the coal dust out. Then Tina brought a hammer and nailed pieces of red cloth up at the little window for curtains. The girls brought in two old chairs, a broken-down couch and a table for furniture. Dede put old bottles and broken dishes on the table and Tina brought a can of old coffee grounds that Mama had saved for her. Hilda poured water on them to make "play coffee."

Suddenly a loud rapping was heard at the coal shed door. The girls opened it, and there stood Jeff with Virgil Tucker on his back.

"Give us a sandwich!" begged the boys. "We're hungry!"

Cousin Trig came running up, with Cliff Crouse on his back. "Give us something to eat!" the boys cried.

"Go away! Go away!" Hilda came out with the broom and chased. The boys went galloping away, with Dede and Tina at their heels. Then the girls came back to rest. "Those mean old boys!" they said.

From the house Tina brought the big old rag doll that Grandma had made for her when she was little. It was named Annabelle. Tina was making a bed for the doll when she heard the whistle of the afternoon train. *Who—o—o—o! Who—o—o—o!*

"Tina! Tina!" called Mama. "Come, help get the clothes in quick! The train is coming."

The girls ran out to help as Celia and Mama rushed to take the clothes off the lines, so they would not get covered with cinders. Mrs. Bryant came out and helped too.

Choo—choo—choo! The long train moved slowly through the valley, puffing smoke and scattering cinders as it went. Tina and Hilda and Dede grabbed armfuls of dry clothes and ran with them to the back porch. They stood on the back porch and waved to the engineer, who waved back.

When the excitement was over, the girls ran to the playhouse, where a surprise met their eyes. Everything was upset. Chairs and table were turned over, dishes and bottles were spilled. Only the red curtains were still in place. Tina could hardly believe her eyes.

"It was Peggy Murphy, I bet!" said Hilda.

"No, it was those boys," said Dede.

"Where's my doll? Where's Annabelle?" asked Tina.

There was no sign of the doll in the playhouse. The girls ran out to look. The boys were nowhere to be seen. They ran over to the Murphys and saw Peggy up on the porch roof.

"What you doin', Peggy?" asked Tina.

"Gettin' my poor cat down," said Peggy. "That mean old dog Queenie chased her up here last night, and she's afraid to climb down."

"Peggy! Peg Murphy!" called Mrs. Murphy from the window. "You come right down off that roof before you fall and break your neck!"

It was clear that Peggy knew nothing of the damage in the playhouse, so the girls came back again. There in the bushes beside the coal shed they found Annabelle. Tina looked the doll over. She was dirty and her clothes were torn.

"Let's play she's dead and have a funeral for her," said Tina.

"Oh, that'll be fun," said Dede.

They found an old cardboard box and filled it with rags. They put the doll in and closed it. They picked wild flowers and stuck them on the box with pins. They dug a hole, put the box in and covered it with dirt. They sang hymns and put flowers on Annabelle's grave.

After the funeral, Tina brought Bright Eyes out from her shed, and they rode the pony round and round the yard.

"Where'd you get that pony?" asked Peggy Murphy, coming up.

"Gramp gave him to me," said Tina.

"He's just an old wore-out mine pony," said Peggy. "He's no good or your gramp would a sold him for three hundred dollars."

"He's good enough for me," said Tina. She slapped the reins and trotted on. Hilda, running behind, shouted back, "You're just jealous, Peggy Murphy, because you can't have a ride!"

"Dede!" called Mama from the porch. "It's time for you to go home. Aunt Effie will be looking for you."

Dede turned to Tina. "Let's dig Annabelle up first."

Tina jumped off Bright Eyes, took a shovel and dug. The girls shook the dirt off the doll, fixed the furniture in the playhouse and put the doll to bed. Then they came out and closed the door tight.

"I'll get a lock and lock it," said Tina, "to keep those bad boys out."

It was wonderful not to have to go to school any more. School was out now, and the children were enjoying the freedom of summer.

One day when Tina went on an errand to the company

store, she rode Bright Eyes. All the children along the way begged for rides, but she said she had to hurry home. As she came past the Tuckers' house, Virgil came out with Jeff.

"Give us a ride!" begged Virgil.

"No," said Tina. "You boys tore up my playhouse."

"We'll do it again if you don't let us ride your pony!" said Jeff.

Tina shook her head. She slapped Bright Eyes on the back and went bouncing down the street. Looking back, she watched the boys start off in the opposite direction on their bicycles. Queenie was following them.

"I wonder where they are going," she said to herself.

She went to the store and did her errand. She rode on home and soon forgot about the boys, for Hilda Krupa was waiting for her. The little Hurley girls, Betty and Barbara, were there too.

"Let's go down to the creek," said Hilda. "I'm hot. Let's go wading."

"Oh, the creek's dirty and our mamas don't want us to get wet," said Tina.

"But they're not washing coal today," said Barbara. "The mine's been closed for two days. The water will be clean."

The chance was too good to miss. The girls ran down across the back lot.

Arbutus Creek ran in a deep gully behind the row of houses not far from the railroad track. At Linden Number

3, they pumped water out of the mine, used it to wash coal at the tipple, then dumped it into Arbutus Creek. So the beautiful wild flowers that once grew there had died, and the banks were covered with black slimy mud. On days when the mine did not operate, in a single evening, the water, fed by live springs, would clear up. The children liked to play in the creek on Saturdays and other days when the company did not run coal at the mine.

The water looked clean and cool, so the girls were soon wading. The June sun shone hot and bright on their backs.

"You push me in and wet me," said Hilda to Tina, "and then I'll pull you in!"

Tina laughed. "I'll blame you if Mama scolds me."

Oh, what fun it was to splash and jump in the creek. The girls threw water on each other and got soaking wet. Even though the water looked clean, the bed of the creek was thick with coal sediment, so the girls came out black. They looked at each other in dismay.

"You're black as coal," said Tina to Hilda.

"You look like a coal miner," said Hilda to Tina.

"We all look like coal miners," said Betty and Barbara.

The sky clouded over and a summer storm came up. It began to rain and the wind began to blow. The girls ran back to the Wilson house as fast as they could go. Now they were wetter than ever.

"You look like drowned rats," said Mama, laughing. "I've got some bath water ready."

Hilda and the Hurley girls ran on home, while Tina took a bath.

Supper was ready and Daddy was waiting. Mama went out on the back porch and called Jeff, but he did not come.

"Where did Jeff go?" she asked Tina.

"I saw him at the Tuckers' when I came from the store," said Tina. "He and Virgil wanted to ride Bright Eyes, but I wouldn't let them. They rode their bikes up Slate Dump Hill. I don't know where they went."

"The rain is over," said Mama. "Go out and see if you can find him."

Tina ran up the road. She stopped at the Bryants', the Hurleys' and the Murphys', but no one had seen Jeff. Then she came to the Tuckers'.

"I haven't seen Virgil since noon," said Mrs. Tucker. "He ate quickly, then said he was going out to play with Jeff. They took their bikes and went off somewhere. I expect they'll be back soon."

Tina went home. "Mrs. Tucker says the boys will be back soon," she reported.

"It's getting late," said Mama. "I wish Jeff would come."

"Queenie's gone too, Mama," said Tina.

"Oh, she tags everywhere with Jeff," said Mama.

Chapter Nine

LOST

MEANWHILE, when Jeff and Virgil left Tina, they rode on up over Slate Dump Hill and came into Crabapple Hollow.

"You go home, Queenie!" called Jeff to his dog.

Twice he stopped and threw stones, but the dog kept coming.

"Queenie's sulky and mean," Jeff told Virgil. "She won't mind only me."

"She's not minding you now," said Virgil.

"Oh well, let her come," Jeff said. "She'll soon get tired and go off home."

The boys passed the Crouses' house and called for Cliff. Cliff and his mother came to the door.

"Why don't you stay here and play?" Mrs. Crouse asked.

"We told Trig we'd come over in the holler," said Virgil. "Aw, come on, Cliff."

"My bike's broke," said Cliff.

"Can't you walk?" asked Jeff. "We'll ride slow."

But Cliff and his mother went in and shut the door.

"He's an ole Mama-baby," said Virgil as they went on.

The boys stopped at Sammy Blagg's house, and found him chopping wood in the yard.

"Come on over to Crabapple Holler, Sammy," called Virgil, "so we can beat you up!" All the younger boys in the coal camp hated Sammy because he was a bully and liked picking on them.

"I'll take you on one at a time and tear you to pieces!" said Sammy, but he did not come. He went back to chopping wood.

The boys went on and at Grandpa Ferris's house, Grandpa hailed them. "Where you boys off to?"

"Goin' over to Trig's house, Gramp," called Jeff. He turned to Virgil. "Let's hurry, so he don't start askin' questions." They rode on.

Crabapple Hollow was a valley between two mountains and had a dirt road that followed a small brook. There were houses on both sides, with vegetable gardens and small fields of corn between. When the boys came to Uncle Chick's house, Trig met them at the gate.

"I thought you were never coming," he said.

"We had a little trouble," said Jeff. "The other guys backed out and wouldn't come. Cliff Crouse said his bike was broke down."

"He's too lazy to think of walking," said Virgil.

"Where's Sammy?" asked Trig. "This was to be our chance to clean up on him."

"He was scared to come," said Jeff. "Even if he's bigger than we are, he knew all of us together could whip him. That really scared him, so he didn't come."

"Well," said Trig, "three's enough, I s'pose. I've got everything ready. Did you bring your hatchet, Jeff?"

"Yes, and it's brand new," said Jeff. "Daddy bought it for me when he went to Mapleton last week." He pulled the hatchet from under his belt and showed it proudly.

The boys went to a shed behind Trig's house. Trig had hard-shell bank caps for Jeff and Virgil. He wore a cloth cap himself. He had a miner's carbide lamp and a package of matches.

"Where'd you get it—the lamp?" asked Jeff.

"Uncle Jack gave it to me," said Trig.

"Is it any good?" asked Virgil. "Bet it's wore out."

Trig lighted the carbide light to show the boys, then put it out. "Let's go," he said. "It's late already." He brought his bicycle and they started out.

"Trig! Trig!" someone was calling.

Trig turned and saw his sister Dede running out after him.

"Where you boys going?" called Dede.

Trig pedaled faster. "Let's not answer," he said. "Let's pretend we didn't hear. She don't need to know where we're going." He looked around later and saw Dede going back into the house.

The boys rode past the houses to the head of the hollow,

and at Trig's suggestion, hid their bicycles in a tangle of bushes at the bottom of the mountain.

"Nobody'll find them there," said Trig. "Nobody will guess we're up here at all."

Trig knew just where he was going, and Jeff and Virgil followed. It was a rough, hard climb up the mountainside, but Trig called it a trail. The boys pushed brush and trees aside, clambered over rocks, and crawled on their knees. Sometimes Jeff chopped off a branch to get by.

"Where you takin' us?" growled Jeff. "There's no trail here. Nobody's been up this mountain in a hundred years."

"Aw, gee! This is no fun, Trig," complained Virgil. "Every step I take I slip back two steps, so I'll soon end up at the bottom."

"Keep comin', boys," said Trig. "Just wait till we get to the top."

"I want to be a miner," said Jeff, "not a mountain-climber."

"You can be a miner if you get to the top," promised Trig.

Fallen branches blocked the way and had to be chopped. The boys climbed, crawled and pulled themselves up, getting scratched and bruised in the process. It took more than an hour to get to their goal.

"Well, here we are!" said Trig.

A dog yelped near by. Jeff looked and there was Queenie. She had followed them all the way up the mountain. He gave her a pat, wondering how she had made it. "Good girl, Queenie!" he said.

Ahead was the portal of an abandoned mine. Above a lot of fallen rocks, the old cement face could be seen.

"There used to be a fence here," said Trig, "but somebody tore it down. The fence was supposed to keep people and animals out." He grinned.

Off at one side was an old slate dump dropping into the valley, with a water hole behind it. The boys went over to look.

"The water's crystal clear," said Jeff, looking down.

"It's real deep too," said Virgil. "Let's have a swim. It won't be cold on a hot day like this."

"No," said Trig. "We're goin' in the mine. That's what we came for."

They came back to the portal but it was blocked by fallen rocks.

"How we gonna get in?" asked Jeff. "It's closed up."

"I'll show you," said Trig. "I been here before."

Trig lighted the carbide lamp, exchanged his cap for Virgil's hard-shell and put it on. He led the boys to the fan entry, pushed some rocks and brush aside and made his way in. The two other boys followed. The daylight at their back soon faded as they went farther in. They walked a short distance, then came to a place where the headroom was low.

"Down on your knees, boys!" said Trig. "Here we go!"

Trig was the smallest of the three boys, but the most daring. It was his idea to explore the mine, so he became the leader.

The old mine was a big one and had been closed down for over five years. The roof timbers had rotted down and some passages were filled with fallen rock and slate. When the boys came to rusty coal-car tracks, they knew they were in the main hallway. Headroom was low here, so they had to hunch over.

"Maybe we'll find a shuttle buggy," said Virgil. "Then we can take a ride."

"Who'll push it?" asked Jeff.

"We should a brought Bright Eyes to pull it," said Virgil, laughing.

Now their eyes were getting accustomed to the darkness. The inside of the mine was black with a darkness that had never known daylight or the brightness of the sun. Even so, the boys could see nothing ahead but the feeble circle of light that shone from the lamp on Trig's cap.

"Why didn't you get lamps for us, too?" asked Jeff.

"I thought you'd have sense enough to bring your own," said Trig.

"You never told us to," said Virgil.

Trig had been pushing ahead eagerly and excitedly. Suddenly he got tired and stopped to rest awhile. He waited for the other boys to come up. They sat quietly talking, when they heard a rustle of movement.

"What's that?" asked Virgil.

"A bat or a rat," said Trig.

A light yelp came, and there was Queenie with her tongue out, panting.

"A dog, you mean," said Jeff. He took Queenie on his lap. "You found us, didn't you, old girl?"

"Gee, it's spooky in here," said Virgil. "Let's go back out. I've seen enough. This is no fun at all."

"Don't be a quitter," said Trig. "We haven't even started exploring. I came this far alone, the other time I was up here."

Jeff was ready to leave too, so in spite of Trig, the boys turned around and found their way back through the fan entry. They came outdoors to daylight again, but a storm had come up and it was raining hard.

"We'll have to stay inside to keep dry," said Jeff.

They went part way in, fooled around and waited. Then they came back to the entry. It was only drizzling now. Jeff went outside and looked around.

"I think the storm's over," he said. "Gee, boys, there's a snake."

On top of the cement face of the main portal lay a snake curled in a circle.

"Gimme your ax, Jeff," said Trig. He climbed up and killed the snake. Then he went in the fan-entry again. "You guys coming?" he called. "I said I was going to explore this mine, and I'm gonna do it."

"Let's go back in," said Virgil.

Virgil went first and Jeff followed. They crawled for a while and Trig said, "This is as far as we came before."

"No, it's different," said Virgil. "I didn't hit my head on the top so often."

"Well, there's miles more to explore," said Trig. "Come on. Maybe we'll find a treasure or something. Besides coal, there's gold and silver and all kinds of precious stones imbedded in rocks . . ."

"We might get lost," said Virgil. "Let's go back."

"Aw, come on," coaxed Trig. "If you don't come farther in, I'll put my carbide light out."

"Then we wouldn't know where we were going," said Jeff.

"So you better stay with me and the light," said Trig.

They crawled on. The headroom was getting lower.

"Say, this sure was low coal in through here," said Jeff. "The miners had to lie down on their stomachs to dig it!" Jeff was not enjoying himself much, but he tried to be cheerful.

The boys laughed. Then Virgil said, "The roof must have fell, that's why it's so low here. It might fall still more."

"This is no fun," said Jeff.

"We've come far enough," said Virgil. "Let's go back. I know all I want to know about the inside of a mine."

"No, no, come on," said Trig. "We're not halfway in."

Jeff and Virgil did not want to be quitters, so they kept on following where Trig led.

"We'll soon come out on the other side of the mountain," promised Trig. "That's where they used to take the coal out, don't you remember? The tipple's over on the Kelton side, down by the railroad track. We'll come out there and go home by the railroad."

"But we left our bikes on this side," said Jeff.

Trig kept stubbornly on, but they did not come to an opening. No signs of daylight appeared. Queenie came part way with them and then disappeared.

"Queenie's gone back out," said Jeff. "Queenie's got sense."

"Queenie's got more sense than Trig's got," said Virgil. "Trig, are you taking us out on the Kelton side?"

"Sure," said Trig, "as soon as I find the opening."

"I want to go back to the side where we came in," said Jeff. "Our bikes are down at the foot of the mountain."

They came to a wall of coal and could not go farther.

"Now we've got to go back," said Jeff. "What did you bring us here for, Trig?"

Trig knew now there was no way out ahead. He knew now they were lost, but he would not admit it. "Just follow me," he said, trying to be brave.

They turned and started back. Trig tried all the different entries, but they all led to dead-ends and they had to come back. Queenie had not gone out after all. She kept coming up to Jeff, barking, and going away again. Once she got hold of Jeff's overalls and tugged.

"Let me alone, Queenie," said Jeff. "That dog's crazy—she keeps pullin' at me. Gee, I'm thirsty . . ."

They came to a pool of water and they all drank, even though they knew it was dirty.

"You're lost, Trig! I know you are!" said Virgil in a scared voice.

Trig started to threaten the boys again, but now all his bravado was gone. "No, I'm not lost," he said, but his voice trembled.

Queenie pulled at Jeff again, then she started toward the pool. Jeff put his arm in the water and it was deeper than he could reach. The dog swam through the water and left them.

"Maybe Queenie knows the way out," said Virgil. "Sometimes dogs are smart and know more than people do."

"Not that dumb Queenie," said Trig.

"We can't swim after her through that water," said Jeff. "It's over our heads. Where do we go now?"

Trig started off in the other direction. He came to an opening eighteen inches high. He was so thin, he crawled through easily, but the two other boys had a tight squeeze. The going

was rough now. The top had fallen, the rocks were slanting and water kept dripping off the roof. It fell on their backs, covered only by thin T shirts, and made them cold and wet. Trig's carbide lamp had a blaze only a quarter inch long. It shone for only about two feet ahead and did not help much.

Suddenly Virgil called, "Gosh! My foot! I'm caught!"

While sliding down over some rocks, his foot became wedged between two of them. He tugged and tugged, but could not get it out. Tired and frightened, he began to cry.

"Don't be a cry-baby," said Jeff.

Trig and Jeff came back to help. They unlaced Virgil's shoe and took his foot out. Then Virgil pulled the shoe out of the crack and put it on again. It was a tennis shoe, soaking wet. The boys tried to go on again, but were tired and discouraged.

"Trig Ferris!" said Jeff. "We're lost and you know it! You brought us in here—now you show us the way out!"

Trig did not answer.

"I know I've crawled thirty miles," said Virgil. "I'm getting hungry, it must be supper time. Oh, what'll my mother say?"

Queenie found them again and came up, barking.

"Shut up, you crazy dog!" said Trig crossly.

No one, least of all Trig, guessed that the dog was trying to lead the boys out of the mine. They kept on crawling and crawling.

At last they came to a big cement face inside a wide hall-way. It was higher here, so Trig opened a half-rotted door and went inside. There was a box in the room with boards on it. Trig read the words FIRST AID, and knew it must be the old First Aid room of the mine. Perhaps they stored the powder here.

Trig read the words and the next minute the carbide light went out. That was the last straw—Trig's courage left him. Tired and exhausted, he fell to the ground and refused to talk.

Outside the door, Jeff told Virgil, "Don't go in there. If we go in there, they'll never find us."

Virgil whispered, "Do you think they'll come for us?"

Jeff said, "Sure! My dad will come," but in his heart he was not so sure. How would Dad ever find them way off in an abandoned mine on the top of Deerfoot mountain? Jeff had been told so often to stay away from old mines, his dad would not think of looking there.

"Jeff," said Virgil, "I wish we hadn't hid our bikes. They'll never find them back of those bushes. They'll never guess we came up here."

"Even if they find them," Jeff said, "they'll think we went swimming in the slate dump pond . . . and got drowned!"

Both boys were near to tears now. They were lying down, too tired to move. But worse than fatigue, they were sick at heart.

"How are we ever gonna get out?" asked Virgil.

Jeff gulped. "I don't know," he said. Inside, he was praying for guidance.

"Hear that?" asked Virgil. "It's rats gnawing. They make tracks as big as a dog's. We'd better not go to sleep. They'll come and bite us."

The boys sat up and made noises to scare the rats away. Then Jeff sniffed a strange smell. "GAS!" he cried, jumping up.

"There's gas coming from that door!" he said. "It's coming from in there where Trig is. No wonder he went to sleep so quick. That place is full of gas—we've got to get Trig out."

Jeff and Virgil made their way into the room.

"Where's the light, Trig?" but Trig did not answer.

It was so dark inside, they had to feel their way to Trig. The carbide light was out and Trig was sound asleep. They had a hard time waking him. They shook and shook him, but he would not waken.

"We got to get out," said Virgil. "There's gas in here. It'll kill us if we breathe it."

"What do I care?" said Trig. He was awake now, all right.

He refused to get up. He kicked his feet against the wall and cried hysterically. He swore and laughed and cried and called the boys names.

"Get hold of his feet, Virgil," said Jeff. "I'll take his head and arms."

Together the two boys tugged and pulled. They brought the fighting, protesting boy out through the door and pushed it shut again. They dropped him on the ground.

"Now what we gonna do?" Virgil turned to Jeff.

It was Jeff now who had to do the deciding.

"We'll stay right here," said Jeff, "until they come for us."

He remembered the sharp rocks that had scraped his back and he was worried for fear the men could not get through. But he did not speak of it to Virgil. There was nothing to do

but to wait and hope for the best.

Trig was quiet again. Jeff and Virgil lay down by his side and tried to sleep. Water dripped on them, gnats stung them and a cold, freezing wind blew across them. They lay there listening to the rats. They hollered until they got hoarse, hoping someone would hear them. They rested, then they hollered again. But only an echo came back.

At last they quieted down and slept.

Chapter Ten

RESCUE

"Has Queenie come back?" asked Daddy.

"No, she's been gone all afternoon," said Mama.

Supper was over, but it was still light. Mama sent Tina out again to look for Jeff. Tina put on her sweater and ran up the road. She went again to the Tuckers' house, but Mrs. Tucker said the boys had not come. Mr. Tucker was away, working in a mine and boarding through the week at a town twenty miles away.

Tina ran up the hill and stopped at Grandpa's house. Grandpa told her the boys had passed by on their bicycles soon after noon.

"Jeff told me they were going to Trig's," said Grandpa.

So Tina hurried on over into Crabapple Hollow. At Uncle Chick's, Aunt Effie and the girls knew nothing. Aunt Effie was not worried at all.

"Oh, they'll be all right," she said.

"Which way did they go?" asked Tina.

"Up to the head of the holler," said Dede. "I saw them. They had bank caps on their heads."

Tina ran down past all the houses. She asked the people

she saw, but they had not seen the boys. The old man who lived in the last house said, "I saw some boys go up the mountain long about noon."

"Did they come down again?" asked Tina.

"I don't know," he said.

Tina turned to go, discouraged.

"There's an old abandoned mine up there . . ." the old man said. But Tina did not wait to hear.

She thought of the time that Uncle Jack took her and Jeff inside Linden Number 3. He had told Jeff never to go in an old mine. Old mines were full of gas which might explode. Jeff would never go in an old mine . . . but fear clutched at Tina's heart. What if he had forgotten Uncle Jack's warning? What if he had gone in the old mine on top of Deerfoot Mountain? Tina ran down the road in the hollow as fast as she could go.

Ahead she saw a man coming. It was Daddy and she put her hand in his as he came up. She told him what the old man in the last house had said.

"Those scalawags!" said Daddy. "Tina, you go back to Aunt Effie's and wait there for me. I want to see if I can find the boys' trail before it gets dark. Tell Aunt Effie to phone Mrs. Bryant and send a message to Mama. Tell Uncle Chick where I've gone."

Tina hurried down the road.

Walter Wilson had no trouble finding tracks in the bushes

at the foot of the mountain, and he soon located the boys' bicycles. From there, he followed their trails of scuffed and broken branches up the mountainside to the mine entrance. There he saw their footprints leading in and out of the fan entry. Had they gone in and come out again? The prints led across the old slate dump to the pond. Walter Wilson stood and looked at the deep water, questioning. Had they fallen in? Or had they gone back and entered the mine?

He went back to the entry himself and walked inside. He tracked the boys to a low place, but could not get through himself because he was too big. He called their names at the top of his voice, but got only an echo in reply. He backed out again. He was a heavy, thick-set man and knew he could not get through the tight places, where the top had fallen. He would have to go for help. He felt sure the boys were inside the mine.

He came down the mountain, went to Uncle Chick's house and told him what he had found. Aunt Effie had been telephoning. Soon Mrs. Tucker drove up, bringing Mama and Mrs. Bryant in her car. Then Uncle Jack came with Grandma and Grandpa Ferris.

The men stood at the gate and talked.

"I don't think they are in the pond," said Daddy. "I think they're in the mine. They're lost and can't find their way out."

"Dede saw them go up the road with bank hats on," said

Uncle Chick. "I figure they went in about one o'clock, and it's nearly six now."

"Five hours is a long time under the ground," said Daddy.

Grandpa Ferris shook his head. "That old mine is full of gas," he said. "The sooner you start a search the better."

"We'll have to get some men and go in from both sides or we'll never find them," said Uncle Chick. "That's one of the biggest mines around here." He turned to Jack. "Go get old Uncle Grimsby—he worked in that mine years ago and timbered it. He'll know his way around."

"Don't lose any time," said Grandpa. "We may be too late already. Better call the Rescue Squad and the mine inspectors. I'll send someone to get carbide lamps and flashlights."

Uncle Chick went in the house and did the telephoning.

Lost in the mine! The women could not believe it. Mama and Mrs. Tucker cried in each other's arms, while the children stood around, frightened. Aunt Effie, fussed and excited now, began telephoning the neighborhood. The news spread like wildfire. The telephone kept ringing as people called back to ask what they could do. The Mapleton newspaper reporter phoned to get news, but there was none to give him except that the boys were lost and believed to be in the mine.

As darkness fell, all the houses in Crabapple Hollow were lighted up from top to bottom. Cars and people came and went. The search party had climbed up the mountainside

and a crowd gathered at the head of the hollow. At the time
that the men entered the mine on the Crabapple Hollow side,
another group, led by Uncle Jack, went in on the Kelton side.

At Uncle Chick's house, Aunt Effie and Mrs. Bryant fixed
refreshments, but no one wanted to eat. Dede and Cindy
begged Tina to come and play with their dolls. But Tina
shook her head and sat down by Mama on the couch.

When the boys had not been found by seven-thirty, Mrs.
Tucker telephoned her husband and begged him to come
home.

"That mine has not been worked for so long," said Aunt

Effie, "the least jar will cause a slate fall."

"Oh, but don't imagine the worst," said Mama. "Maybe the boys never went inside at all."

"The men feel certain they did," said Grandma. "Otherwise they'd a been home by dark."

Tina looked at Mama. "Are they gonna find them, Mama?" she asked.

Mama brushed aside her own tears to reassure the girl.

"What can we do?" asked Tina.

"Just sit still and wait," said Mama.

"And ask God to take care of our boys," added Grandma.

So the women and children folded their hands and prayed.

Jeff roused from his sleep and wondered where he was. Then he knew that he had not dreamed it. It was true—he was lost in the mine. He was dirty and wet and chilled through. Trig and Virgil were lying beside him, sleeping. It was black, black-dark in the mine. How long had they been in there? Was it night or day?

Suddenly Jeff heard a noise. It sounded very loud in the stillness of the mine. Something was moving. Was it a rat —a rat as big as a cat? There were fantastic stories about mine rats, but what was it Uncle Jack had said? "A rat is the miner's best friend!" He had told Tina to come and feed "our little pets." So a rat was nothing to be afraid of. Jeff tried to reassure himself.

In the quiet, Jeff thought about Tina and her bad burn and

long illness of last winter. He remembered how she loved the mine ponies, and he was glad that Grandpa had given her Bright Eyes. He never fought or quarreled with Tina, the way some boys did with their younger sisters. He and Tina were always the best of friends, even if he was her brother. What was Tina doing? Was she still riding Bright Eyes, the way he saw her last? Or, was she out hunting for him, wondering why he did not come home? What time was it? Was it night or morning?

The noise came again, closer this time. It was something moving. Jeff shook with fright, but called out bravely, "Hey! Hey there! What is it? Who are you?"

He waited, his heart in his mouth.

Then he heard it. A voice replied, "That you, boys?"

"Yes." Jeff gulped. He could hardly speak. Someone had found them. Who was it? He saw a light flickering.

Jeff reached over and punched Trig and Virgil.

"Boys, wake up," he said. "Somebody's found us."

"Who? What?" asked Trig.

"Who's there?" sang out Jeff, his fears fading away.

"It's me—Uncle Chick!" said the man.

Virgil said, "Is someone coming?" and could hardly believe it.

They waited, then Uncle Chick came through a narrow place, sliding on the slate, feet first. Soon he was down where the boys were.

Uncle Chick acted as if he were used to finding lost boys every day.

"Boys," he said. "I'm glad I found you, but don't ask me how I got here. We'll just have to take a shot at the moon to get out of here. I haven't the least idea which way to go, but come along with me anyhow."

The boys got up and crawled after him.

"We thought you were all dead from black damp," Uncle Chick said.

The boys laughed nervously.

Uncle Chick kept on talking. "We saw your tracks to the water hole. Did you go in for a swim?"

"No," said Jeff. The boys did not feel like talking.

"I don't know how you boys got over here," Uncle Chick went on. "You must have crawled over piles of slate and waded water holes up to your neck!"

Still the boys had nothing to say.

Going back was not easy, although Uncle Chick led the way. In some places he had to hold onto the top rock with his fingers and pull himself through. The boys pulled each other. In one place, they made tracks two inches deep in dry coal dust, which they did not remember on the way in. But at least now, they had Uncle Chick's flashlight to guide them. Once they saw some pieces of copper, which they picked up to take out with them, but Uncle Chick made them throw it down.

"The other men are waiting," said Uncle Chick. "I was the smallest and skinniest of the men, so they made me go all the way in. I had to go in crawling—scraping top and bottom."

After a time, they came to the place where the other men were waiting. "Did you find them, Chick?" they called out.

"Sure!" said Chick. "Alive and kicking too!"

The other men began to laugh and joke. All the tension was eased now that the boys had been located.

At last the whole party came out of the mine. It was dark

outside now, nine o'clock at night. Jeff's daddy and Grandpa Ferris were with the waiting men. The men were both glad and mad to see the boys. They began to tease. "You boys are gonna get the worst whippin' you ever had in your lives for a stunt like this!" they said.

The boys hung their heads ashamed.

Suddenly Jeff remembered his dog. "Where's Queenie?" he asked. "She went in the mine with us."

"Forget the dog," said Daddy. "You come on home now. Queenie will find her way out all right."

"Oh, and my hatchet!" Jeff felt at his belt. "My new hatchet—I left it in the mine . . ."

But nobody cared about the hatchet, even if it was a new one. The important thing was to get the boys home as quickly as possible.

At the bottom of the mountain Uncle Chick's truck was waiting. The boys climbed up in the back. Their hearts were light now, for they were going home. Trig found a box of groceries with a bunch of onions on top. He handed them to Jeff and Virgil. The boys were so hungry, they ate the onions and said they tasted good.

Two mine inspectors drove up just after the boys were brought out. After hearing the news of the boys' rescue, they drove to Kelton and went in on the Kelton side to find Uncle Jack's search party, to tell them the boys had been found. Afterwards, it turned out that the boys had been located near the Kelton exit. The fresh air blowing in from this exit had saved their lives. Uncle Jack's party took chalk to mark their way with arrows, to avoid getting lost, themselves.

At Aunt Effie's house, three mothers were happy to see their boys again. They put their arms around them and cried.

Everybody crowded round. "Hey, boys, what happened?" they asked.

Trig had recovered enough to speak for the other two with something of his old bravado. "We had a good time exploring . . . but we thought we'd never get out."

The people laughed, but Jeff turned to Virgil and said, "I don't think it's funny, do you?"

Virgil shook his head. He still could not talk.

The boys were a sad sight. Their blackened faces were streaked from crying, they had cut places on their backs, hands and knees. Their overalls were cut through at the knees. Their thin clothes and tennis shoes were soaked and they were shivering with cold. They wished the people would go away and let them alone.

Uncle Chick wanted them to say something, so he asked, "Well, boys, do you still want to be miners?"

Virgil found his tongue at last. "I'd rather take a hundred whippings than stay in there," he said.

"I'd rather be put in jail for the rest of my life than be in there," said Jeff.

"I still want to be a coal miner," said Trig. "I'm not scared. I'll take me a rope and tie it and go back in . . ."

Everybody laughed. The boys went into the house.

"Come on, Trig! Come out to the woodshed!" called Uncle Chick. "I'll warm you up in no time."

But Grandma Ferris spoke up. "No—no whippings!" she said. "After all they've been through, these boys have been punished enough. They have learned their lesson, I'm sure."

The other women agreed.

Virgil's daddy did not return until after Virgil was already at home and in bed asleep. He said, "Well, since it was such a narrow escape, I won't whip him. I'm thankful he's still alive."

Mrs. Bryant drove Jeff and his family home. Jeff was so starved he went first to the kitchen, and Mama fed him right away. Then she washed him and put Mercurochrome on his scratches. His clothes were black and he had coal dust in his hair.

Jeff sat down on the couch and tried to tell the family about it. But he could not talk, for the tears kept coming fast.

"I don't ever want to go in a mine again." That was all he could say.

"He's too nervous to talk," said Mama. "I'll give him some nerve medicine so he can sleep."

"Put him to bed right away," said Daddy. "No telling what all that poor kid has been through."

Before he dropped off to sleep, Jeff called out, "Has Queenie come home?" He was worried that the dog had been left in the mine.

The next morning Queenie still had not come home. Jeff slept until noon, although visitors crowded the house and kept coming and going.

That evening, Jeff's daddy said, "We can't leave Queenie in the mine. We'll have to go and get her out."

Jeff shook his head. "You can't get me to go anywhere near that old mine again."

"Uncle Chick will take you," said Daddy. "He won't let you get lost. He was up on the mountain this morning and he heard the dog barking inside. He tried to coax her out but she refused to come. She thinks you boys are still inside."

"She tried to bring us out," said Jeff, "but we were too stupid to come. She kept pulling at my pants' leg . . ."

"You can't let her die in there," said Daddy. "She's had no food since yesterday morning. She's *your* dog. She won't mind anyone but you. You'll have to go inside and call her."

So the three boys went into the mine again the next day, not voluntarily, but to bring the dog out. This time they followed safely *behind* Uncle Chick, tagging at his heels, so there was no danger of losing their way. Queenie's barking grew louder and louder as they came closer.

Jeff called her, "Queenie! Queenie!" and she came running up to him. She wagged her tail and jumped on him, excited and happy. He took her in his arms and carried her out of the mine.

"Queenie deserves a gold medal!" said Mama, when they

came home.

Jeff, Trig and Virgil had had the adventure of their lives, and the people in Crabapple Hollow and Linden were not going to let them forget it. They had to tell their story over and over until they grew tired of it. They saw their names in the paper, and they were teased unmercifully.

When Jeff went to the company store, Mr. Frazier came rushing out to meet him. "Hi, Jeff!" he called. "Let's go inspect the mines!"

All the clerks crowded up and laughed at him. The Linden boys were even worse.

"What shift are you on, Jeff?" asked Cliff Crouse.

"Take me in the mine with you, Jeff," said Sammy Blagg. "I want my name in the paper too."

Jeff was glad to get home again. Only Mama seemed to understand.

"We were just exploring, Mama," Jeff told her. "We weren't doing anything bad."

"I know," said Mama. "All boys are curious. It could have happened to any boy."

Mama told the others to stop talking to Jeff about it, because it made him so nervous.

"I want him to forget it," she said, "but I reckon he never will as long as he lives."

Chapter Eleven

WEDDING

Here we come!
Bum, bum, bum!
Where you from?
Pretty girl station.
What's your occupation?
What's your trade?
Lemonade!

ALL the girls were playing in the Wilsons' yard, divided in two lines facing each other. As one side acted out its "occupation," the other side tried to guess.

"Digging coal!" called Tina.

Her guess was right, so the others ran, and Tina's side tried to catch them.

It was the day of Uncle Jack's wedding. He was getting married to the schoolteacher, Helen Sanford. All of Miss Sanford's pupils had come and were playing in the yard. They were waiting for the bride and groom to come from the preacher's house. While they waited, the girls played games and the boys ran around, riding on each other's shoulders piggyback.

At last several cars drove up and out of the first one jumped Uncle Jack. He was dressed in his Sunday suit and had a white carnation in his buttonhole. His shoulder and arm were well now and he no longer needed a sling. He helped his bride out, and they went into the house, where all their friends and neighbors were waiting.

Tina ran up and kissed her new Aunt Helen. Tina was used to the name now and glad to have her not only for a teacher but as a member of the family. Aunt Helen was dressed in white. She had some flowers in her hair and a bouquet of white flowers tied with ribbons in her hand.

The children crowded into the house. A long table was set with many dishes, and the women were bustling about getting everybody seated. The children were shooed outside again and told they must wait for the second sitting. They began to play again. Tina chose *Little Sally Ann* and took her place in the center of the ring. The children began to sing:

> Little Sally Ann, sitting in the sand,
> Weeping and crying for a little man.
> Rise up, Sally, dry your eyes,
> Turn to the East, then turn to the West,
> Then turn to the one that YOU LOVE BEST!

They played for a long time.

Then suddenly there was great excitement. The bride and groom came running out of the house, followed by all the people. Aunt Helen had changed her clothes. Now she was dressed in a going-away suit of dark blue, and she wore a smart little hat with a feather. Uncle Jack had two suitcases in his hands. The people threw a shower of rice and confetti

over them, as they climbed in Uncle Jack's car and drove away.

The children waved as long as they could see them. Then the car turned the corner and wound up the hill to Mapleton.

"Where are they going?" Hilda Krupa asked Tina.

Tina shook her head. "It's a secret," she said. "Aunt Helen and Uncle Jack wouldn't tell anybody. They are not supposed to tell where they go for a honeymoon."

"I bet I can guess," said Peggy Murphy. "I bet they went to Charleston."

Tina closed her lips tightly. How did Peggy Murphy know more than she did herself?

It seemed very quiet at home that night, after all the people went away. Mrs. Bryant and Aunt Effie stayed to clean up the kitchen, and then they, too, went home. Left alone, Tina was surprised to see tears in her mother's eyes.

"But I thought you were glad . . ." she began.

"I am," said Mama. "I'm glad, but sad too, to lose my baby brother. I looked after Jack for so many years, it will be hard to get along without him."

"Isn't he coming back?" asked Tina.

"No," said Mama. "They're going to live in Charleston. He has a job there."

The children were surprised to hear the news.

"But he can't . . ." said Jeff. "I mean, there are no mines in Charleston."

Daddy spoke up. "Uncle Jack is giving up mining," he said. "He's young, he has opportunities, he can find other work to do."

"It's all the fault of that teacher . . ." Mama started to say something, then closed her lips, seeing the surprise on the children's faces. "Aunt Helen, I mean. She got her way with him at last. She was determined he shouldn't be a miner."

"Can you blame her?" asked Daddy. "Just remember what happened to old Ben, my buddy—her father."

Mama tried to smile. "No, I don't blame her. At least now, Jack won't get his back broken in a slate fall and have to spend the rest of his life in a wheel-chair like poor old Ben. At least now, Jack is safe . . ."

"Until he gets smashed up in a car wreck, driving at seventy miles an hour!" Daddy laughed.

"Aunt Helen will take care of that, too!" said Mama.

"I hope she does," said Daddy.

"Are you going to stop being a miner, too, Daddy?" asked Tina.

"Now, Tina, you know better than to ask that," said Mama.

Jeff turned to his sister and said, "Of course not, silly!"

"Now that the mine has opened up again . . ." began Daddy.

"You think it's never going to close down!" said Mama. "There's no bigger fool of an optimist than a coal miner."

Daddy laughed. "At least the miner has learned to look on the bright side of things," he said. "At least I have work again and I am thankful for that. Coal mining is a dog's life, but I guess I'm hardened to it. I'm a miner by trade and I never want to be anything else." He turned to Tina. "Once a miner, always a miner," he said.

After the flood, it had taken some weeks to get the mine in shape again. Then the men were called back, and operations had started on a larger scale than before.

Hope returned to the little coal camp. The fear that the mine might close permanently faded away, and the miners' families took heart again. Even with the dwindling of the coal supply and the frequent shutting down of the mines, even with the moving of many families out of the area into homes of their own and other occupations, the miners were filled with hope. In spite of the periodic ups-and-downs in the coal-fields, in spite of the non-existence of other work near by and the consequent trapped sensation in the minds of the miners' families, which colored all their life and thought, there remained a hard core of miners who chose never to be anything else, and who would keep on being miners as long as they lived.

Walter Wilson was one of these. He lived through and accepted the hardships and hazards of mining as a necessary part of his life. His wife and family accepted them too, though Mrs. Wilson would, perhaps, be the last person to admit it. There was a real challenge in the work. For the miner depended for survival upon technical ability, physical fitness, mental alertness and loyal teamwork, all commendable qualities. His very directness, straight-forwardness and lack of pretense stemmed from the nature of his work.

When the white birches grew on the slate dump, the fire burned them, but they always grew back again. Long after all of man's mining operations have ceased, trees and bushes will take root and grow, to cover the gaps in the hills and the unsightly slate dumps. Only Nature can heal the scars made by the hand of man. And so the white birches became the symbol of the miner's perennial hope.

That evening, when Jeff and Tina were riding the ponies in Grandpa's pasture, they talked quietly together.

"Tina, you shouldn't ask Daddy if he's going to stop being a miner," said Jeff.

"Why not?" asked Tina.

"Mama don't like coal mining—the women never do—but Daddy has to do it," said Jeff. "He don't care if Mama don't like it, he has to do it anyway. He has to work somewhere. He's a born miner—he could never work outside a mine."

"But he might get hurt," said Tina. "Mama don't want him to get hurt—that's all."

"Of course not," said Jeff. "But Daddy is careful. In all the forty years that he's been mining, he's never had but one lost-time accident—that time he lost his two fingers."

Tina looked thoughtful for a moment.

"Are you going to be a miner, Jeff?" she asked.

Jeff's face grew sad for a moment.

"I was scared to death when I was lost in the mine," he said soberly. "I was so scared, I think I'll never be scared again as long as I live. Getting lost up there has taken all my fear away."

"You won't be afraid to be a miner, Jeff?" asked Tina.

Jeff did not answer directly. He began slowly as if weighing every word. "Virgil says he'll never be a miner, and Trig says he won't be afraid to be one. And as for me, I'll be a better miner just because I was lost in the mine."

"But you said you'd rather stay in jail for the rest of your life," said Tina, "than go in a mine again."

"That's what I said at first," Jeff went on. "But I've had time to think since then."

"You still want to be a miner?" asked Tina.

"Yes," said Jeff. "I'm a born miner like Daddy, I guess."

THE END